GARZA TWINS ✹ BOOK ONE

THE SMOKING MIRROR

GARZA TWINS ✳ BOOK ONE

The Smoking Mirror

DAVID BOWLES

The Smoking Mirror

All Rights Reserved

ISBN-13: 978-1-925148-64-0

Copyright ©2015 David Bowles

V2.3 US

Printed in Palatino Linotype, Maya Culpa, Cuprum

Melbourne, Australia

IFWG Publishing International

www.ifwgpublishing.com

ACKNOWLEDGMENTS

The Smoking Mirror has its roots in the culture I grew up in along the South Texas-Mexico border. The places described are real, though I've used them in a fictional way. Many of the supernatural creatures in these pages first appeared in the stories I heard at the knee of my grandmother, Marie Garza, or from other relatives and friends through the years.

I owe my familiarity with Monterrey and Saltillo to my wife's family, whose willingness to love and guide me in tough moments of my life has left me forever in their debt. Also instrumental in this book's genesis have been the hundreds of students that passed through my care in my fourteen years as a teacher. I learned as much from them as they from me.

Certainly, *The Smoking Mirror* would not exist were it not for my wife and children, who are eternally supportive of my writing and put up with my weird hours and impromptu readings of key scenes. The same should be said for the writing community of Texas and the Southwest, especially Guadalupe García McCall, Xavier Garza, René Saldaña, Jr., Malín Alegría and Jason Henderson. Their coaching and friendship made this project easier.

Finally, in crafting my fictional version of the Mesoamerican Underworld, I have drawn from several primary source documents, like the *Florentine Codex* and the *Popul Vuh*. The reader should note that I blended elements of both Aztec and Mayan mythology together, and any major differences from the actual beliefs of the indigenous peoples of Mexico arise from my own creative choices.

For readers unfamiliar with Spanish, a glossary is included at the back of the book.

To Angelo and Charlene, the best friends a dad could ever want.

CHAPTER ONE

C arol was awakened by the prickle of the morning sun on the back of her neck and a persistent itch against her left cheek. Opening her eyes with a groggy yawn, she was startled to see grass spreading all around. She lifted her head and realized she was lying in her backyard. Her arms were stretched out before her, and there between her hands sprawled a dead jackrabbit.

"What the...?" Carol muttered, pulling her hands away with a start and sitting up. She noticed that her nightgown was ripped in several places. Scrambling to her feet, Carol ignored her confusion and rushed to the house. She slipped through the back door, down the hall, and into her bedroom. Her mind whirling with possibilities, she changed into her school uniform, hiding the torn gown beneath her mattress.

In the bathroom, she checked her face in the mirror for any signs of panic or fear. There were none. The last six months had taught her to hide those emotions well. Her dark eyes peered coolly from her reflection as she smoothed her hair. *Nothing wrong with me, nope.* She smirked at herself.

Crossing the hallway to her twin brother's room, she flipped on the light and announced, "Time to get up, Johnny."

A sleepy voice murmured from beneath a pillow, "Is Dad up?"

"I don't know. Haven't checked. But it's 7:15, and you need to hurry up."

"Alright, I'm going."

Her twin untangled himself from the sheets, which were twisted and untucked after a typical night of tossing and turning. With the awkwardness common to all twelve-year-old boys, he bumped and lurched his way to the bathroom.

Her stomach knotting for a moment, Carol walked through the kitchen to her dad's study. As she had predicted, he was curled up like a child on the sofa that faced his desk. His multiple diplomas and awards hung on the wall, crooked and forgotten. On the floor beside him was a nearly empty bottle of liquor.

I'm not going to cry. Not going to. She laid a tentative palm against his shoulder. "Pops? You going to work today?"

"Hmm? No, no." He squinted at her, his hazel eyes bloodshot and sunken. "Go on to school, Carolina. I'm fine. There's money on the desk."

Wanting to hug him and tell him she knew he wasn't fine, that she wasn't fine either, that her heart and Johnny's heart were just as broken as his, Carol instead swallowed hard, grabbed five dollars from the desk, and quietly shut the door.

She and Johnny walked the kilometer to Veterans Middle School in silence, till he looked at her oddly. "Did you dye your hair or something?"

"No, Moron, I didn't. Why?"

"I don't know. You look, you know, different."

"You're hallucinating. I look the same as ever. Get over it."

Her brother glared at her in irritation. "Yeah, well, whatever." They'd reached the parking lot, and Johnny hurried ahead, melting into the wave of students getting off a bus.

Why can't we talk anymore? We're always angry and rude now. Why can't we just move on? But Carol knew that families didn't just move on from loss with such ease. Ms. González, her counselor, had talked about the grieving process often enough that Carol had memorized all the catch phrases: it's best not to hide the pain; you need to talk to someone about your loss; it takes time to reinvest yourself in life…

Yet the problem wasn't the loss itself. What was tearing her family apart *was not knowing what had happened.* There was no closure, like Ms. González said there needed to be. *How can I grieve when I don't know her fate?*

Six months ago, Carol and Johnny's mother had disappeared. And no one knew how, why, or whether she was even alive.

The tragedy was made even worse by the fact that their father was coming apart at the seams, believing that he had done something to make her want to leave. Johnny was certain she was dead. And Carol…

She isn't dead. She didn't run off. Someone took her. I don't know how I know it, but I do. Someone took her and they're hurting her and there's nothing I can do to stop it.

On top of everything, Carol was certain she was going crazy. Waking up with a dead hare in her hands was clear evidence of her imbalance. Popping into the library, she logged on to a terminal and searched for *sleepwalking*. A quick review of the results showed that it could be caused by stress, both physical and psychological. There was without doubt a high level of stress in

3

her life: losing her mother, watching her father—the man she most admired in all the world—spiral into depression, feeling her twin draw further and further away from her...

But the jackrabbit? She had no clue.

Despite her exhaustion, she went through the motions in her classes, but the image of the hare kept popping into her head. From time to time she seemed to scent the sharp odor of fresh blood. The most frightening thing was that the smell made her mouth water.

***

unning. Under the stars. Ghostly trace of jackrabbit through sandy soil. Crouching, extending claws. Pouncing as a form darts into the moonlight. Sinking teeth deep into soft flesh...

"Carolina Garza!"

Carol jerked her head up, glancing around at her giggling classmates. She had fallen asleep. Her math teacher, Mrs. Ramos, looked at her with concern and disapproval. "Carolina, you can't be falling asleep in class. Do you need to go splash some water on your face, *m'ija*? Take the pass and go wake yourself up, okay?"

Wooden pass in hand, Carol headed to the restroom. She rubbed water on her face, digging her knuckles into her sleepy eyes, and then looked at herself in the mirror.

Her eyes flashed an inhuman yellow, and she gave a little scream.

"Carol?" Pushing through the door came Nikki Jones, Carol's best friend. Heart racing, Carol glanced back at the mirror and saw her normal eyes, wide with fear and bloodshot.

"Uh, hey, Nikki."

"You okay? I saw you through the window on the door, so I came to say hi. But then I thought I heard you scream."

"Nah, I was just…just yawning. I didn't get too much sleep."

"I texted you last night."

Carol sighed. "They cut off my cell. My dad didn't pay the bill."

"Ah, that sucks. Hey, I gotta get back to class, but you're going to go with me in June, right? To my church's summer camp?"

Though a part of her didn't want to go, Carol had decided that she needed to get away from her house, get her mind on something different. She felt horrible about her dad's depression, so she still hadn't asked him. "I'll talk to my dad about it tonight, okay? Tell you tomorrow for sure."

The rest of the school day was pretty uneventful. There were just a few weeks left before summer vacation, and students and teachers both had their minds on the near future. She and Johnny walked back to the house in silence, Carol's eyes flitting toward quick movements in the long grass and scrub. Jackrabbits. She thought they were cute, hated it when feral dogs or cats killed one. Why in heaven's name would she pick up a dead one, even when sleepwalking? Or was it dead when she grabbed it? But that was crazy. Carol couldn't catch and kill a wild hare…wouldn't even if she could.

The silence went on as the twins did their homework, and it continued uninterrupted while they sat at the dining table, eating the hamburgers their dad had brought when he came home. It was unbearable, that silence. Carol wanted to scream, to rage against it before it filled all of them with emptiness. Her father had always been the one to shatter that ugly absence, with a laugh or a song. She needed him to be her protector, like he had always been. But Oscar Garza had surrendered to silence.

Something was on his mind, Carol could see. It looked like he was trying to figure out how to give them news they wouldn't like. It was almost exactly the same look he'd had on face when he informed them of their mom's disappearance.

After a minute or so, he began to speak, soft and low, in his serious professorial voice. "Kids, I know how hard the last few months have been on you. And I know I haven't really been there for you like I ought to be. It's just," his voice cracked a little, "it's just that I love your mother very, very much, and my soul can't deal with her absence, with this betrayal."

"Mom didn't betray us," Carol interrupted. "You don't know that she did."

He nodded, staring with an absent gaze at a spot on the wall behind her, and continued on as if she hadn't spoken. "I need more time to get through this. And I'm neglecting you, I know it. So today I spoke with your *tía* Andrea..."

"No way," breathed Johnny.

CHAPTER TWO

Dr. Garza ignored his son and continued. "I spoke with your *tía*, and she's agreed to look after you this summer while I get some professional help."

Johnny Garza couldn't believe what he was hearing. Aunt Andrea. In Monterrey. Mexico. For three long months.

Carol made a small, strangled sound. Johnny turned to look at her in surprise. For the first time since their mother's disappearance, his twin sister had begun to cry.

"Way to go, Dad," he snapped, lurching to his feet. "That's some amazing parenting right there."

He stomped off to his room, slamming the door and throwing himself on the bed. Anger and loss boiled inside him. He grabbed tablet and earphones, choosing the darkest dubstep songs he could find and blasting beats into his mind until exhaustion overwhelmed him and he slipped into sleep.

Johnny moved through a watery barrier and found himself in a dark place. From all around came the sound of dripping water. He felt a sense of dread, of something evil lurking in the dark. His eyes became adjusted to the dimness, and he made out a form. It was his mother, her arms outstretched, a look of desperation and pain on her face. "Johnny," she moaned. "Johnny, come find me. Find me before he hurts me again."

That was when he woke up, startled by the wrongness of the vision. His mother had never called him *Johnny* in his nearly thirteen years of life. For her, he was always *Juan Ángel*, and if she called out to him, it was in Spanish: *ven, m'ijo; ven acá. Come, son. Come here.*

But this was the third time he'd had such a dream since his father's announcement: the darkness, his mother's voice, the certainty that she was alive but in danger. It meant something. As crazy as it sounded, Johnny believed she was reaching out to him. He just had no idea how to even begin searching for her.

He revealed none of this, of course, to his handful of friends when he arrived at school. But as they sat together in the cafeteria that morning, he at last shared the bad news about his summer vacation

"Mexico?" exclaimed Jaime Villanueva, slurping down his orange juice. "You serious? We'll be lucky to see you again next year with all the cartel violence and stuff."

"Yeah, that's pretty lame, dude," his best friend Robert Blanco muttered. "Was going to invite you to swim in our pool, but...yeah."

Cody Smith—son of the mayor and Johnny's rival since kindergarten—took great pleasure in the news.

"Dude, you don't even speak Spanish!"

"Yeah, I do, Cody. Just not around you poor monolinguals."

"Whoa! Johnny Garza just used a big word...somebody mark it down on their calendar."

"You're an idiot, Cody."

In a town like Donna, Texas, news gets around fast. The following day, he was bombarded by questions by people he didn't even know. With every new question or probing remark, Johnny felt a strange pressure building inside him, like nausea or fear or anger. Everything—from Cody Smith's smugness to the teachers' sympathetic looks—began to rub him raw.

"Aren't you worried about getting kidnapped?" a random cheerleader asked.

"No. Aren't you worried about how tight your freaking ponytail is?" Johnny snapped in return.

"I hear the police have no leads yet," some smug eighth-grader commented out of nowhere. "That must be tough."

"Not as tough as walking around with a face as ugly as yours, you freak," Johnny growled.

"My mom says your dad's seeing Dr. Flores, the shrink. She's a receptionist with the dentist next door to him." This was from Lorenzo, a kid who was always asking to borrow money from everyone. "I see a shrink, too, you know."

"Really? You don't say. Wow. Never saw that one coming."

After a few days of this, people stopped approaching him at all. He could see he was alienating his few true allies at Veterans Middle School, but a part of him just didn't care anymore. All he could think of was his mother, alone in the dark, and how helpless he was to do anything about it.

He found himself in the dark again. He could sense his mother nearby, crouching and afraid. There was silence, thick and black, and then he heard a voice thrumming in the very rock around him: *I will break her, boy, grind her into dust. Do you have the will to stop me, you mewling knave? I am waiting.*

Leaping to wakefulness, Johnny tumbled from his bed, chest heaving, shirt soaked in sweat. Overcome with powerless rage, he slammed his fists against the floor. "What is happening to me?" he rasped into the deepness of the night. He could not get that horrible voice out of his mind. It seemed to rattle his very bones as he lay sleepless. It squeezed at his heart as he tried to scrub the dream away in the shower. It followed him all the way to school, mocking him.

I am waiting.

Later that morning, as he was slouching his dazed way down the hall, he accidentally bumped into Miguel 'Mickey Mouse' Maldonado, a thug who'd spent the last three years in eighth grade. Everyone knew that Mickey Mouse was brother to a member of a local gang that styled itself 'Southside M13.' Not the kind of guy to get physical with.

"Sorry, dude," Johnny muttered.

"Sorry nothing, *güey. ¿Qué te crees?*"

"*No me creo nada.* I'm just a guy, walking down the hall. Was an accident."

Maldonado stepped closer to Johnny. "*Conque hablas español, bolillo.*"

"I'm not white, man. *Güero, sí.* But not Anglo. Not all the way."

"I'm asking you? No, *ese.* I already know who you are, anyways. You're the *vato* who his mom like ran off with some *sancho*, and now your dad, *se está volviendo loco*."

The pressure in Johnny's chest threatened to explode at any second. "My dad," he said between clenched teeth, "is not going crazy, *imbécil*."

A girl with pencil-thin eyebrows and black lipstick shook her head. "Oh, man, you just screwed up."

Mickey Mouse's eyes had narrowed to slits. Somehow, Johnny sensed the movement before it even began: the right fist swinging up from below, faster than Johnny should have been able to avoid. But he did, moving his chin back so that Maldonado's blow took the wannabe gangster off balance. Instinctively, Johnny's own right hand shot out and grabbed the older boy by the throat. At the same time, he used his own weight to pin Maldonado against the lockers with a ringing thud.

"You want some of this, wankster?" Johnny growled, his vision going red with fury. It was as if someone else had taken over his mind and body. He couldn't even think clearly about what he was doing. "I will take your flunky, useless carcass out and feed it to the coyotes if you EVER speak about my family again."

Pushing himself violently away, Johnny left the older boy sputtering and rubbing his neck. The entire hallway had gone silent, and other students just stared at him with their mouths open as he headed to class. A security guard, who like always had just been standing by and watching, clapped him on the shoulder. "Way to go, Garza. But now you'd better watch your back. That guy's an animal."

Johnny didn't reply. His breathing slowed, and he thrust his black bangs out of his face with a trembling hand. As he entered class, his mind slowly unfroze. *An animal? Well, maybe I am one, too.*

It turned out, however, that there was no need for Johnny to watch his back. At about 3:15pm he was called to the office and told to take his backpack with him. In the reception area sat his father, Carol standing in front of him with an angry look on her face. When he saw Johnny, Dr. Garza stood up and gestured.

"Come on, John: your cousin Stefani is waiting to accompany you two to Monterrey." He set his hand on his shoulder and began guiding him toward the exit. "I know there's a week of school left, but I went ahead and withdrew you. They didn't want to, but I had them classify you as migrants."

"Migrants?" Part of Johnny didn't even care anymore. Something had his mother. It was waiting. He wasn't going to find it in school.

"Just a formality. You know, use the system to our advantage."

"Ours or yours?" Carol's eyes were blazing.

Their father said nothing more as they walked to their SUV and climbed inside. The afternoon May sun glowered with hostile heat; the air slowly baked the landscape, and the vinyl seats defied the power of the air-conditioning to quench their searing touch.

Okay. You're waiting, whatever you are. Well, I'm coming. I don't know how, I don't know where. But I'm on my way, you monster. And I'm getting my mother back.

CHAPTER THREE

The drive to Monterrey was nerve-wracking. Carol kept imagining that at any moment the Zetas—those violent, ex-military drug traffickers—were going to stop the bus and get everybody out. *We'll end up in one of those big graves they dig. They'll find us months from now, no head, no hands.*

Stefani, who insisted on speaking English so she could practice, laughed these fears off. "No way, Carolina. Those Zetas, they aren't going waste their time stopping this bus. I choose the cheap one, you see? Very bumpy ride. No movie."

Carol couldn't argue with that. The bus was miserably warm, and the bathroom stunk like road kill. She tried to read a book, but Stefani kept chattering away about American movie stars and singers, none of whom Carol knew anything about. Johnny was pretending to be asleep in the seat in front of them, so she had no choice but to nod politely and give one-word responses to the older girl's comments.

Eventually Stefani sighed and got serious.

"Carolina, I know that this is hard for you. When my dad left us, I cried and cried. It's not easy. Maybe you think that you have the fault, but no. Our parents, they decide for their selves what they're going to do. It doesn't mean that they don't love us."

Carol tried not to be upset. Her cousin was just trying to

comfort her. But she was very tired of everyone's assumptions. "Look, Stefani. It's easy for you and other people, including my dad, to believe that Mom ran off. But check the facts. She didn't take any clothes, no toothbrush, no hair-iron...nothing. That woman is *always* in front of a mirror. Why would she leave without taking all her make-up and expensive clothes? It doesn't make any sense."

Stefani nodded. "*Ya veo.* I see. But Uncle Oscar told to my mom that there was no signs of...struggle. All doors locked. But her car was in the parking...the driveway, yes? Could be possible she had...with all respect...a boyfriend? Maybe with more money? Could be that he pick her up, promise to buy her new things?"

At that, Johnny sat up, his fake sleep forgotten. "That's stupid. Mom wouldn't do anything like that. It's pretty obvious what happened. She walked to the store, and she was grabbed. Same thing happened at that gas station three years ago. Woman was pumping gas, and some gangbangers took her. Family never heard from her again...till they found her body near the river."

"Shut up, Johnny." Carol's face felt hot. She wanted to reach out and claw at his stupid smug expression. "Mom's not dead. I...I can feel that she's not."

Johnny's hazel eyes misted over for a second. "Well, it's not doing anyone any good, all this talk about stuff we can't change. Why don't you two just change the freaking subject?"

But the conversation was already dead. They traveled the last few hours in silence, jolted miserably by the uneven highway. The mountains loomed closer and closer, almost menacingly. The grungy industrial metropolis of Monterrey finally seemed to spring up out of nowhere all around them; gray and cracked concrete broken here and there by graffiti or the bright colors of the occasional home that struggled to be different. Carol noticed Johnny staring intently at the buildings and elevated metro lines. Like their mother—a respected sculptor who had exhibited work in Austin, Dallas and Mexico City—Johnny was fascinated by design and construction. His dream was to be an engineer when he grew up...he had spent much of his free time since their mom's disappearance using a computer-aided design program to plan all sorts of buildings and bridges that Carol had to admit were pretty ingenious. As they passed the Arch of Independence, her brother craned his neck to stare at the statue of Victory poised at its very top. Victory was flanked by bronze eagles, and she hoisted a globe in one hand while the other gripped a broken chain. *One of Mom's favorites. Even though she'd left her country, she was still proud of its history.*

As they passed the stately city hall, museum and basilica that flanked the *Macroplaza* at the heart of Monterrey, Carol reflected on her parents' passions. Her father's doctoral dissertation had been on Mexican history, and he'd expanded those ideas into a series of well received books over the past decade. *It's like Mexico is part of what held our family together. Even though Johnny and I are pretty Americanized—*gringolizados, *Mom always said—we love the old country, too. Me with its history, Johnny with its architecture and music.*

At the bus station, Aunt Andrea hugged them tightly and fussed over how much they had grown. Carol had to bite back tears: Andrea looked so much like her mom, had the same raspy voice, used the same phrases. Seeing her was a reminder of the special friendship that had developed between mother and daughter, and Carol's heart ached like it hadn't in weeks.

The four of them piled into Andrea's sedan and weaved through the dense afternoon traffic to Colonia Tecnológico, a once-exclusive borough of Monterrey that was slowly fading as the wealthier families either moved to even more ritzy neighborhoods or emigrated to the States, fleeing narcoviolence. Andrea parked in front of an apartment building whose two towers made it look like an artificial version of the saddle-shaped Cerro de la Silla, the hill that rose majestically on the horizon.

That evening, Carol helped her aunt and cousin prepare dinner. Andrea's kitchen was a magical place, full of colors and spices and fantastic cooking utensils. The three of them joked together about how stupid boys and men could be sometimes, telling each other anecdotes of particularly knuckleheaded behavior. Andrea, who had just divorced her third husband, was especially gifted at pointing out men's defects. For a while, Carol could simply forget, relishing the company of women.

But that night, as she lay in a narrow bed across the room from her brother, her dreams returned. She was roaming the unfamiliar neighborhood, guided by new smells. There were many dogs, she could tell, all of them competing with each other. A sense of calm confidence flooded her. They would not dare approach her. They were slaves to men, made docile and stupid. Street canines believed themselves free, but they lived off men's garbage and handouts.

She soon caught the scent of an opossum. She hated the vile creatures. But she was hungry, so she gave chase. Cornering the hideous, slippery beast, she rushed it, her teeth sinking into its back, cracking its spine...

Sometime later, she snapped awake, an unpleasant taste in her mouth. She padded to the bathroom and scrubbed her teeth. In the mirror, her eyes glinted strangely. She spent a few minutes combing tangles from her hair, which had frizzed out wildly in all directions. Returning to her bed, she tried to fall back to sleep, but adrenaline kept her eyes wide open. She heard her brother stir, sit up, mutter a curse. Quick footsteps indicated that he rushed to the bathroom and after a few minutes, slipped outside. Finally Carol sensed him moving around in the kitchen. Checking the time on her otherwise useless smartphone, she saw that it was already 6:00am, so she got up and went to join him.

"Dude," he said apologetically as he poured milk over corn flakes, "I didn't mean to wake you up. Sorry."

"Nah, that's okay. I was having weird dreams, anyway." She grabbed a banana and sat down across the table from him. "You alright?"

He nodded, his mouth full. "Yeah, sure," he said after a couple of seconds. "I guess it beats watching Dad get drunk every day. It's just..." He glanced down the hall, toward Andrea's bedroom.

"She's a lot like Mom, huh?" Carolina peeled the banana and took a bite. "It's tough to forget with that voice in your ears."

"Who said I'm trying to forget?"

"Oh, come on, Johnny. You don't even want to talk about it."

He leaned back in his chair. "That's because, like I said, we can't do anything. You girls, I swear. You think you have to talk about your feelings and stuff. Why can't you just *feel* your feelings and leave it at that, huh?"

"Because, you moron, talking about them makes them easier to deal with."

"Well, whatever. I don't think they *should* be easier to deal with. We lost our mom, Carol. I *want* to feel that. I *need* that pain." His voice hitched. "It keeps her alive for me."

Carol decided not to argue. An accustomed silence fell across the table. Eventually, Andrea and Stefani woke up, made coffee, and outlined plans for the day that included visiting a museum and a park. With the pretext of throwing the kitchen trash away, Carol went to the parking lot, trying to figure out why her brother had slipped outside before breakfast. She didn't find anything until she opened the trashcan and saw a bit of clothing peeking out from under a bag. Carefully, she reached in and pulled a shirt free. It was Johnny's favorite, purchased at a *Nortec Collective* concert he and their dad had attended two years previously.

It was in shreds. In fact, it looked like it had been clawed to bits.

And it was stained with blood.

arol didn't say anything to Johnny about the shirt. Their aunt dragged them all over the city, buying them more clothes and even paying to get service for their phones. After they got back to the apartment, Carol spent several slower-than-normal hours on the Internet, getting caught up with the goings-on back in Donna, messaging her friends and downloading a few more tunes. But as bedtime got nearer, she realized she had to investigate.

I'll stay up and keep an eye on him. There's no way that happened to him in bed: the sheets are fine and there's no blood in the room. He must've snuck out.

They both finally lay down at nearly midnight, after watching a couple of dubbed movies on TV. Carol didn't have to wait long for her brother to start softly snoring; like their dad, he was one of those early-to-bed, early-to-rise kind of people, different from Carol and her mom, who stayed up late and slept until noon if they could. As she lay on her side, she surfed the net with her phone to occupy her mind. Nearly an hour passed in this way.

She had just begun researching unexplained abductions along the border when she heard a snarl from Johnny's bed. Flipping her phone around so that its light fell on her brother, Carol squinted in the gloom. Johnny was twisting strangely in his bed, his back to her. Suddenly he bolted upright, his arms shooting out from under the sheets.

Both hands were covered in fur, and claws jutted from every finger.

Stifling a scream, Carol pulled up the camera app on her phone and started taking photos. Johnny's head snapped around at the clicking noises, and she watched as his face changed. His nose widened and flattened; his jaw protruded painfully, causing a grimace that revealed sharp, feline teeth; his eyes glimmered redly with each flash from the smartphone. With a muted growl, he leapt from the bed and crawled out the open window. Carol hurried to look outside and saw him dashing off, hunched over as if wanting to get down on all fours. She switched her phone to record and grabbed a few seconds of footage before he disappeared into the night.

Quietly, trying to calm her ragged nerves, Carol made herself a cup of *café con leche* and sat on her bed, awaiting her brother's return. She looked up *werewolf* and *wolf-man* and everything else she could think of. *I can help him. I know I can.*

Despite all her intentions, Carol had begun to doze slightly when Johnny bounded through the window and curled into a ball on his bed. His tail twitched as he closed his eyes.

His tail? What the…

Sleep overcame the transformed boy, and slowly his body reverted to its more human shape. This time he had not torn his clothing.

Can he remember stuff from his normal life? Did he take more care this time? Her questions would have to wait until morning. By now it was nearly 4am, so Carol lay down and drifted off. She was not troubled by dreams.

"**C**arol, wake up, dude."

Blearily, she sat up. Johnny was lacing up his Converse hi-tops. He smiled at her, and for a moment, she seemed to see that feral face superimposed on his features.

"Johnny," she said as he got up. "Wait. Lock the door."

"Uh, excuse me?"

"You need to see something, and I don't want Andrea walking in."

Johnny raised an eyebrow and scratched his temple.

"Photos on my phone, dude," she explained when he made a funny face.

"Ooookaaaayyyy." He locked the door and sat down on her bed. "What are these top-secret pictures of, anyway? Your cute friend Nikki?"

"Oh, my God. You are an idiot, aren't you? Look, you wouldn't believe me otherwise...I found your shirt in the trash."

Johnny's face blanched. "Wait, I can explain..."

"Hold on. So I stayed up to see where you were going."

"I didn't go anywhere!"

Carol opened up the camera app and accessed the photos. "Oh, yes, you did."

Johnny took the phone and began swiping through the images, his eyes getting wider and wider. "Dude, you totally photoshopped these."

"Yeah. In the middle of the night. On Andrea's five-year-old computer. With my non-existent image-manipulation skills. That's your department, Mr. Computer-Aided-Design. Here, give me that." She found the video she'd recorded of him running off into the night. "How do you explain this then, genius?"

Johnny watched himself rush away like a creature from some 1930s horror film. He set the phone down and ran his hands through his hair. "Holy crap, Carol."

"Yes."

"But it explains a lot. The strange feelings I've been getting, all the shirts I've been ruining..."

Carol thought for a moment about her own dreams, about waking up with the dead desert hare in her hands. She kept all that to herself for the moment. *No reason to make things even more complicated.* Pushing down the suspicion that something strange might be happening to her as well, she nodded.

"Yeah. I don't know...maybe you caught something, maybe you were bitten..."

"Maybe it's a family thing," Johnny finished, almost looking excited. "And maybe Mom's disappearance has something to do with it."

Before Carol could add her thoughts to this line of reasoning, someone tried to open the door.

"Hey, Carolina? Juan Ángel? Open up," Andrea said to them in Spanish.

Johnny unlocked the door. "Sorry. Force of habit."

Andrea waved his apology away. "Kids, my sister just called from Saltillo. Your grandmother wants to see you."

Picking sleep sand from her eyes, Carol tried to remember *Abuela* Helga's face. Four years ago she had suffered an embolism; another one had followed six months later, leaving her paralyzed on one side of her body, confined to a wheelchair and barely able to speak. A flush of shame crept across Carol's cheeks as she thought about her grandmother, helpless, needing family to care for her, making do with just *tía* Sandra, the *solterona*, the spinster.

When we came last summer, Mom asked me to go with her. I told her I would just stay at the hotel, watching movies with Johnny. I can't believe how cruel I was. And Mom just shook her head sadly. It must have broken my mother's heart.

Biting her lip to hold back tears, Carol stretched with feigned laziness. "Okay. Are we driving there today? Let me just get dressed."

If Andrea noted anything strange about the twins' behavior, she kept it to herself.

A few hours later, they were travelling west through the Chihuahuan desert, climbing closer to the Sierra Madre Oriental. Saltillo spread before them, stone and concrete and adobe that blended with the surrounding sand and rock. Making their way through busy streets, they passed street vendors whose mobile *puestos* were parked in front of American chain restaurants. *We've invaded, like the Aztecs and the Spanish did before. But this invasion is harder to fight.* She remembered her dad telling her about Comanche warriors striding along the streets of Saltillo in the mid-1800s. The Mexican government had hired former Texas Rangers to hunt that tribe down. *And they've been stuck with us ever since,* she reflected, a little embarrassed. The English names disappeared as they traveled deeper into the city. The ancestral home of the Quintero family stood near its center, in the historical district, a century-old structure of caliche block and clay roofing tiles.

Parking on the street, Andrea led the twins and their cousin into the broad courtyard, where their Aunt Sandra stood waiting for them behind their grandmother's wheelchair. Sandra was short and dark-complexioned: more like her father, everyone said. Carol had never met the General, but photos of the brooding, serious man could be found in most of his children's houses. His widow, once beautiful and tall, now slumped feebly in her wheelchair. Carol moved quickly to embrace the old woman, whose one lucid eye looked at her intensely.

"How are you, Carolina?" Sandra asked with a warm but sad voice. They hugged as Johnny kissed their grandmother's cheek.

"Fine, *tía* Sandra. Happy to see you two. It's good to be with family."

23

Smiling wistfully, Sandra nodded. "Yes, dear, it is. I'm so glad you could visit." She squeezed Johnny, who managed not to smirk. "Here, let me show you how I've redecorated."

She guided them through the roomy home, its normal earth tones accentuated by bright splashes that had to be Sandra's doing. Once the twins were installed in a cozy bedroom on the second floor, Carol and her aunts went into the large grove that formed a semicircle around the house. Shooing away butterflies, they picked peaches to make the creamy dessert that had become a family tradition over the years. Stefani joined them in the kitchen as they set to peeling and slicing the peaches and preparing the crust and the cream. Their talk was light and joyful, but there was an unmistakable undercurrent of loss.

When the dish was baking in the clay oven, Carol went looking for her brother. She found him sitting on a bed in the large bedroom on the first floor that looked out on the grove. Their grandmother Helga was sitting in her wheelchair across from him.

She was struggling to speak.

"Johnny, what's going on? She needs to rest."

"She wants to tell me something, dude. I tried to tell her not to worry, to just relax, but she gets all agitated."

"Ca-ca-ca…" the woman slurred out of one side of her mouth.

Carol stiffened a bit. "You don't think she needs, you know, to be *changed*?"

"No, you moron. Just let her speak, okay? Be patient."

Helga lifted her arm weakly. "*Ca-ca-ca…cajón.*"

The twins looked at each other.

"Does she mean *her* drawer?" Johnny wondered aloud in English.

Carol shrugged. "Well, she was pointing at the dresser." Turning to their grandmother, she asked in Spanish, "Do you want something from your drawer, grandma?"

Almost imperceptibly, Helga Barrón de Quintero nodded her head.

Johnny leaned back, smirking. "Sounds like a job for you. I am not going through *abue's* undies. No way."

Carol sighed. "You started this, Johnny. But fine." Crossing to the rustic-looking chest of drawers, she began opening each one, looking for something that their grandmother might be wanting. The old woman made dismissive grunting noises at the hairbrush, the barrette, the silver handheld mirror.

In the bottom drawer, under a pile of scarves and leg warmers, Carol's hands closed around a thin leather book. She pulled it into the light. Gilt initials spelled out *VQB* across the cover.

"Is this what you wanted?" she asked, turning around. Helga's eye lit up excitedly.

"VQB," mused Johnny, thinking of his mother's two surnames. "Verónica Quintero Barrón? Did it belong to Mom? Is it her bible or something?"

Carol undid the clasp and opened the volume to the first page. In a neat manuscript hand, someone had written the date—13/X/88—across the top of the page.

"13th October, 1988..." Carol looked up at her brother. "I think this is Mom's diary."

Their grandmother, with great difficulty, nodded her head twice, slowly.

"R-r-r-read."

CHAPTER FOUR

As his sister read, Johnny felt prickles of nostalgia along his skin: her voice gradually taking on the rhythms and intonation of their mother's speech. It was like Verónica Quintero de Garza was in the room at that precise moment, sharing her innermost thoughts.

Today Mom told me the craziest thing: like her, I'm a shapeshifter. A nagual. *I didn't want to believe her, but then she shifted into a* jaguar *right in front of me! She was orangey-gold, with a white belly and black spots. Only her eyes were the same light brown, though with a little shimmer.*

Mom shrugged off her pink dress and prowled around for a while, then went into the bathroom. She came out a few minutes later, in human form, wearing a bathrobe.

"What the heck, Mom? How long have you been like this?"

"Since I was your age, Vero. On my side of the family, there is a nagual *born every generation, to the previous shapeshifter, unless she doesn't have children. In that case one of her sisters will bear the new one."*

"But how did you know it was me and not Sandra, Andrea or Carlos?"

"I didn't. Not until a month ago, when I saw you wandering the peach grove."

"What are you talking about? It's been months since I was out there."

"No, Sweetie. You have been visiting it every night for the past five weeks. Hunting."

"You mean...I've been shifting into a jaguar like you?"

Mom shook her head and explained. "It takes time for a nagual to fully transform. At first we begin partially shifting, each change introducing more and more animal characteristics. After a few months, the process is complete. Learning to control your ability is another story, however. What emerges when you transform is your tonal, your beast-soul. Everyone has one, but very few can perceive it. Even fewer can allow it to come forward into this physical world. For most naguales, this is a natural process, like what you're going through. But a small number of sorcerers learn to pull their tonal through their flesh..."

"Wait." I couldn't believe what I was hearing. "Sorcerers? So not only do were-jaguars exist, but witches, too? What else? Vampires? Mermaids? Unicorns?"

Mom smiled at me, not the sort of reaction I had expected or wanted. "Almost all the old stories are true, Vero. But people hunted most of those ancient creatures into hiding or extinction long ago. And were-jaguars? No, that's something totally different. But you're getting me off track. What I'm trying to tell you is that it is difficult to control your tonal. You're not used to having a conscious awareness of that aspect of your being. That's why you don't remember anything about your transformations."

"But...now that I know, won't I start remembering? Won't I be aware?"

"To a small degree, yes. But it takes a lot of practice, Sweetie. I can guide you somewhat, but we're going to have to enlist the help of more knowledgeable folk."

She didn't explain what she meant, but she promised she'd be with me in the grove tonight, in jaguar form. Now that I've jotted all this down, I'm going to try to get some sleep. I mean, close my eyes and let my beast-soul take over. Or whatever. Goodnight.

Johnny leaned forward. His heart was racing, his palms tingling. "Whoa. So I'm a *nagual*, too, huh?" He looked at his grandmother, who smiled crookedly and swiveled her head around to stare at Carol.

"Uh, Johnny...there's something I need to tell you."

Carol's face was flushed, and she dropped her gaze to the tiled floor. Johnny understood right away. "Wait. No way. You, too? Dude!"

"You probably think that this is totally cool, don't you?" Carol had her normal I-don't-approve-of-your-boyish-enthusiasm face on.

"Hello. Of course I do. Are you nuts? We get to transform into big freaking cats. How is that *not* cool?"

"Well, it sounds like *Abuela* Helga was pointing out some pretty major drawbacks back in 1988, Johnny-boy."

"Just keep reading...gah. Girls, I swear."

Narrowing her eyes, Carol continued.

So I remember bits and pieces now. Smells, mainly. Specifically, the smell of blood. The sound of a beating heart. The scent of my mother, racing ahead of me, showing me how to flush a brace of jack rabbits.

This morning she was sitting at the foot of my bed, smiling.

"You're almost completely a jaguar now, when you transform. Do you remember?"

I told her I did.

"Good. Pretty soon we'll take a trip to Monterrey. To visit your cousins. At least," she whispered, "that's what we'll tell your dad. In reality, we're going to visit the García Caves. Some...experts in these matters...can be found there."

"Who, the tour guides? There isn't anyone else living up on Friar Mountain, Mom. It's in the middle of a national park"

"I'm more interested in the folk living inside *the mountain, Vero. But you'll see what I mean soon enough."*

I ignored her cryptic remark for a moment. "Why do we have to lie to Dad, though? Doesn't he know...what you are?"

Mom's eyes got all misty, and she glanced away. "He knows. That's...that's how we met. It was the late '60s, during the student movement: civil rights protests, pro-labor rallies, meetings to promote equality for women. He was a captain in the army then. His men, searching for secret anarchist meetings and so forth, found my mother and some other naguales, *and—oh, Sweetie—they killed them. Then they began to investigate their families. Your dad tracked me down...I was studying at the UNAM in Mexico City. He pretended to be a graduate student. We...I fell for him. He's pretty handsome, you know." She laughed a little. "Anyway, I guess he couldn't go through with...turning me in or whatever. When he told me the truth, I hated him a little. But by then I had no choice. I had to be with him. He could protect me in ways I couldn't protect myself. He made me swear to stop transforming. I never told him it was hereditary, but I'm guessing he knows. We haven't spoken of it in twenty years."*

I was so angry at my dad at that moment. I want to run into his office and confront him, tell the super important Colonel Quintero what I thought of him. But my mother took my hand and stroked my hair.

"It's the nature of things, Vero. Naguales, like other magical creatures, have been slaughtered throughout the history of Mexico. We are blamed for awful tragedies, and occasionally we have been guilty. And that's why it's very important that you never speak of this secret with anyone, not even your siblings. Especially not your father. You can't leave any record of any of our lore, either. It has to be kept here and here." She touched my head and heart.

But I can't keep this inside me. I'll go crazy thinking about it. That's why I hunted up the diary Dad bought me last year (I never wrote in it...never had secrets up until now), and now I'm using it to find relief. I'm excited, I'm scared, I want to cry, I want to laugh. Tonight Mom will be with me again, running free under the silvery moon. I'm going to try to remember more. And when she takes me to the mountain, I'm going to learn everything I can.

Johnny stood up and mused aloud. "The García Caves. Dad said they used to be underwater grottoes, like millions of years ago. Remember how he wanted to take us to see them in fifth grade?"

Carol nodded. "Yeah, and Mom got all panicky and said no. That it was too dangerous or something."

Their grandmother muttered excitedly.

Johnny knelt beside her. "The caves are important, yeah?"

A tear welled up in the old woman's good eye. *"Va-va-va-vayan."*

Johnny nodded and glanced over at his sister, who was flipping through the remaining pages. "She wants us to go, Carol. To the caves."

Holding up the diary, she pointed to a blank page. "There are just a few more entries, and then nothing. Did you catch her, *abue*? Is that what happened? You took it away to protect her?"

Tears were now rolling down their grandmother's face. Before she could attempt to say anything further, Andrea walked in.

"Kids, it's time for…" As her voice trailed off, she rushed to her mother. "What happened? Why is she crying?"

A little panicked, Johnny blurted, "We don't know. We were talking about Mom and she got like this."

"Well, shoo, both of you. It's not good for her to get this worked up. Go wash your hands. Dinner's on the table." She began making soft, reassuring sounds as she embraced the old woman and tried to console her. Carol closed the journal and pressed it to her side as she walked out of the room. Johnny followed.

By the time she was wheeled to her place at the table, their grandmother had grown calm, a peaceful expression softening the lines on her face, making her look as Johnny remember from the early years of his childhood. In a few months he would become a teen, but he suspected he would never be able to forget how his grandmother had fostered his love for building, buying him blocks and Legos, then model kits of buildings and bridges. *She understands me. It was tough, seeing her become an invalid. I didn't want to face it. But now I've got to understand her. There's something important here, and not just that me and Carol are shapeshifters. She needs us to do something. In the caves.*

After dessert, Stefani wanted them to go with her to the movies, but the twins begged off, saying that they were exhausted and wanted to turn in early. They sat down across from each other, on narrow guest beds cushioned with thick *San Marcos* blankets, and said nothing for the longest time.

"We have to go to the caves," Johnny finally said.

Carol nodded. "She definitely wants us to go. I guess you want to learn to master this whole shape-shifting thing, huh?"

For such a smart chick, she can be really dense. "Not just that, Carol. There's something else. Why was Mom scared to return to those caves? I think...I don't know how, but I think we can find out what happened to her there."

"Johnny, those old grottoes are four hours away from Donna. That's not how she disappeared."

Johnny kicked off his Converse high-tops. "Dude, I know that. But maybe there are clues. Or maybe these mysterious 'folk' that Grandma mentioned to Mom know something. Does she ever say who they are in the diary?"

Carol let the pages flip through her fingers. "Nah, the entries stop right before they take their trip."

"Well, we'll have to find out for ourselves. When we head back to Monterrey, let's get Andrea to stop. We'll tell her we want to sightsee."

Carol slid the diary into her knapsack and pulled out her smart phone. "So, jaguars. Yikes. I guess that explains the spots I saw on you."

Johnny reached for the phone, started scrolling through the photos. "Yeah, I can see it now." He paused on a close-up of his transforming face: a broad bridge of the nose, rounded feline ears, golden downy fur ringing his face. "I'm like a *jaguar-man* or something. You know, like the difference between a werewolf and a wolf-man?"

"Ah, yeah, more like jaguar-*boy*. You don't turn thirteen until September. Even then, *man* is going to be a bit of a stretch."

Johnny threw a pillow at her. "Ha, ha. Tonight's your turn, *mensa*. I'll stay up and use my tablet to record you. It's got better resolution than your cheap phone, anyhow. Then we can make fun of how you look, okay?"

T hey made preparations and then hit the sack. It took forever for Carol to fall asleep. *She's such a freaking night-owl.* Johnny had gone down to the nearest *depósito* and picked up a two-liter soda and a bunch of *Gansitos*. He set to munching on the chocolate pastries and swigging the caffeine and sugar-laden drink while sketching a building whose curved ceilings were reminiscent of enormous caves.

Eventually the sugar rush wore off. He struggled to stay alert, but his eyes kept shutting. He would jolt awake with a start, only to find Carol still asleep and still fully human. Just when he was about to give up on his surveillance, however, she growled, and all grogginess left him as he lifted his tablet and pressed record.

Carol was crouching on her bed, sniffing at the air. Pointed ears sat high on her skull, and her jaw had stretched into a snout.

Her arms were covered in gray fur with tan and black highlights or markings, ending in claws that dug into the blanket. She tilted her head and stared at him.

"Uh, Carol, you don't look like a jaguar to me," he muttered, his voice trembling. She snapped her jaws, then leapt from the bed, landing in a crouch on the floor near the open window. Ignoring the ladder they'd propped against the house, Carol dove into the night. Johnny rushed to the windowsill. His sister was loping toward the peach grove. When she reached the first trees, she tilted back her head and howled.

"Dude!" Johnny muttered, flipping the tablet around to record his annoyance. "How come she gets to be a wolf?"

He glanced down again and gasped. A jaguar sat in the sandy dirt, staring up at him. It gestured with its head as if inviting him down. Then it turned and ran after his sister.

Could that be…? His heart racing, Johnny lay down, trying to fall asleep. Adrenaline was coursing through his veins. *This is insane! I need to transform! I've got to blank my mind.* He plugged his earbuds in and dialed up some soothing electronica. It did nothing. His frustration was overwhelming.

And then, finally, he dropped into the dark.

CHAPTER FIVE

acing alongside her brother, their grandmother as a jaguar before them, guiding them. The smell of open spaces, the feel of the moon on her muzzle, the taste of fresh blood on her tongue. The jaguar circling them, drawing them down on all fours. The human girl inside falling further away as the wolf-self comes more fully forward. Seeing the invisible skeins that connect rock, root and claw: the ties that make human friendship pale in comparison.

The jaguar had turned to look at them, her eyes almost human. Then she had turned and run into the mountains. They had watched her disappear in the pre-dawn dark.

Carol awakened to loud sobs. She felt her own cheeks: they were dry. Sitting up, she saw that Johnny was still fast asleep on his bed, curled up like a napping cat. From the ground floor came more sounds of sorrow: a stifled scream, furniture being scraped across tile.

"Johnny!" Her brother snapped awake. "Something's wrong. People are crying and freaking out downstairs."

He shook his head as if to clear a few cobwebs, and they descended together. They found their aunts and cousin in their grandmother's room. Helga Barrón de Quintero lay cold and lifeless on the bed, her body more emaciated than ever, as if some essential part of her had left forever. A smile lay lightly on her lips.

It was her. She ran with us last night. Somehow...she escaped her own broken body. Tears came to her eyes, but she had to fight not to laugh with joy.

"She waited." Johnny's voice was husky with emotion as he leaned toward her. "She could have been free years ago, but she waited. For us. To make sure we knew."

They went to their family, then, trying to console them in a grief they didn't share. *What a burden she carried. And now it's ours, too.*

Hours later, when Uncle Carlos, his wife, and the other relations had arrived, Andrea handed Stefani the keys to her car. "I know it's tough, but you've got finals tomorrow, and we can't afford for you to ruin your last year at prep school. Drive back to Monterrey. Pack me some nice things and my black dress, you know the one. After your exams, drive back. We'll have made all the arrangements by the then. The funeral should be on Wednesday or Thursday."

Carol placed her hand gently on her aunt's back. "Andrea? Can we go with her? We didn't bring many of our clothes with us and we'll need more. We can also help her pack and stuff so she can focus on her studies."

Andrea's face was conflicted for a moment, but Carol put on her most mature expression and waited. After a few seconds, her aunt gave in. "You sure you two will be alright? Lupita will be by to clean tomorrow afternoon—I'll call her and ask her to cook for you while she's at the apartment. I'll get my downstairs neighbor Susana to check in on you, too."

She's actually relieved. What she doesn't need right now is a pair of pre-teens underfoot when she's trying to deal with all this tragedy.

"Thanks, Aunt Andrea. We'll behave ourselves, promise. It'll also give us some time to...digest all of this."

Andrea hugged her tightly. "Oh, baby, I know this must be hard for you, losing your grandmother so soon after—" Andrea concluded the sentence with kisses.

It was impossible to suggest to Stefani that they stop at the caves on the way back. The eighteen-year-old wasn't as devastated by her grandmother's passing as some of the other family members, but she was somber and focused as she drove through the desolate landscape, listening to loud, growly alternative music. An apparent frivolity like exploring the wide expanse of ancient grottoes was not going to fly.

lets wait til shes n school tmrw & take a taxi, Johnny texted Carol.

K. Good idea. Wait, do you have money? she texted back.

no but i saw where andrea keeps stash we can borrow some.

Would it kill you to punctuate?

rly? thats what u r concerned about? id be more worried about why u turn n2 a wolf n not a jaguar maybe u r defective.

She punched him, but it was strange. Pulling out her mother's diary, she read the rest of the entries carefully. One passage in particular caught her eye:

Thank God I've got mom to talk to about this. Eventually, if I have kids, one of them will be like us, and then the three of us can share the secret together. Unless I have twins. Mom says that hardly happens. She says there haven't been twin shape-shifters in centuries.

She handed the diary to Johnny, pointing out the paragraph. His eyes grew wide.

see? theres something about us & maybe moms disappearance is related to it.

Hopefully. We need to be ready for anything, though.

They both spent the rest of the trip researching the caves and lore about *naguales*. A lot of what they found on the Internet was just nonsense, urban legends or embellishments created for non-Hispanics who wanted to use Mesoamerican creatures in their role-playing games and so forth. But there was plenty of information that seemed legitimate. Carol even found a scholarly monograph on shape-shifting sorcerers. Though the researchers treated the beliefs of villagers seriously, it was obvious they thought the Mexicans who believed in *naguales* were just trying to find explanations for tragic deaths in their communities. Still, their interviews of elders in the southern Mexican towns yielded some tidbits of lore. Apparently, it was tough to kill a *nagual* without ritually prepared weapons, but there were many ways to make a sorcerer revert to human form in order to lynch him. Carol had no idea if any of this was applicable to natural-born shape-shifters, like her brother and her, or just to people who used spells to make their *tonal* come forward. She could only hope that the folk in the mountain would enlighten her.

That night was the first during which she was aware of her transformation, though it seemed distant and dreamlike. From deep within her came a pressure, an almost physical *need*. Instead of fighting against the rising sensation, she mentally relaxed, dropping all barriers and inhibitions. A hungry, eager part of her leapt into the gap left by her relinquishing of control. It was her *tonal*, a glowing, vital force that required more than human flesh to inhabit the world. It hooked itself deeply and *molded her*, like masterful fingers pulling at clay. She reached out to the tonal, tentatively at first, but then with excitement, embracing it, linking with it. She saw through its eyes. The former darkness of the bedroom was startlingly clear, and her keen vision was enhanced even more by her powerful sense of smell and hearing, revealing a world she barely glimpsed as a human girl. Every subtle movement around her, every glimmer of light, conveyed incredible amounts of information.

It was dizzying.

Her transformation, as far as she could tell, was complete. She could smell the jaguar on the other bed, could tell that his senses were changing, too. Then he thudded to the floor beside her. They could not speak to each other, but so much could be communicated with gestures of muzzle, ear and tail.

They turned to the open window. The night called to them, and they rushed to answer, leaping into the moonlight.

"**You** two stay out of trouble," Stefani warned as she scooped up the keys from the counter in the morning. "Just hang out here. Surf the Internet, watch some TV, read a book. I'll be back around 2:00pm."

Carol assured her that she'd keep Johnny in check, and Stefani almost smiled at the conspiratorial us-against-them tone.

They let some time pass, then they grabbed their knapsacks and headed to one of the main streets, hailing an *Eco Taxi* and asking the driver to take them to the caves.

"Shouldn't you two be in school?"

"We're American," Johnny answered with a smile. "School's already over for us. We're meeting our parents at the park to explore the caves."

The taxi driver shrugged. "So long as you can pay." Johnny foolishly flashed the pesos they'd taken from their aunt's bedroom; the man nodded, turned on his meter and drove off to the polka rhythms of some *norteño* band on the radio. The twins chatted excitedly in English about their experiences during the most recent transformation, comparing notes and speculating on ways to trigger the shift while they were still awake. Before long, the taxi dropped them at the parking lot near Friar Mountain with Johnny leaving him a generous tip from the borrowed funds. They hiked up the trail a way, then paid sixty pesos each to ride the aerial tramway up the steep slope. After ten minutes of hanging precariously in the air, they walked with a group of tourists into the large principal chamber. The air was comfortably cool, and the great expanse of rock hanging overhead suitably impressive. A guide gathered the newcomers, giving them maps and a choice: the A twenty-minute or one-hour tour. Not sure what to expect, the twins opted for the longer one.

Metal walkways that had been painted yellow led the way from chamber to chamber, each of which had a distinct name. As they moved through the chambers, they were duly amazed at some of the massive rock formations: the 'Christmas Tree', the 'Frozen Fountain', the 'Chinese Tower'. There were walls like melted wax, pools of sterile water, and what was extravagantly called *The Eighth Wonder*: a stalactite and stalagmite that met exactly halfway from the ceiling and floor. Carol saw that Johnny was entranced by the structures, but she could hardly focus on them. She kept looking around, searching for some sign of the mysterious folk in the mountain.

The twins lagged well behind the group they were with. As they mounted another set of rickety metal stairs, Carol noticed some fossils embedded in the rock to her left. As she took a moment to study the ancient sea creatures that had left their mark, she glimpsed something moving in a gap just beyond the walkway. She leaned over the railing, peering into the darkness that lay between two formations. Straining her eyes, she managed to make out a form: a boy, it seemed at first, maybe six or seven years old. But then a glow came from his hands, and she stepped back, startled, bumping into Johnny.

"Hey, watch out, dude! You're going to knock me down the stairs or something."

She ignored his complaints. "Johnny, look."

It was not a boy. It was a small man-like being, pale-skinned, with a shock of black hair and large, widely set eyes. It wore a simple linen loincloth and sandals. In its long-fingered hands it held a rock, the source of the light.

"Come," it whispered. "Over the railing. Quick. Before they see you."

Carol and Johnny stood stock still. The being grew impatient. "Carolina, yes? And Juan Ángel? You're here for a reason. If you want to know what it is, I reckon you'd better climb over the railing this very minute."

They obeyed, jumping across the short space with ease. Carol saw that the little man only came up to her chin. Surreptitiously she sniffed the air, a new habit she was picking up from her shifted existence. He had no smell. Or rather, he smelled of rock and water and sterile sand, like everything else around her.

"Come on then," the little man said in his lilting, old-fashioned way. "The others are waiting."

Carol found her voice. "The other what?"

"The other *tzapame*, Little People. We come to set you on your path. Now, enough dawdling."

He moved quickly through the darkness, and the twins rushed to keep up. After a couple of minutes they came to a solid wall. He placed his hand on a particular spot, chanting strangely in some language Carol had never heard. A section of the wall faded, and the three of them stepped into a dimly lit chamber that was not on the tour map.

It was full of *tzapame*. Some were a little taller than their guide; others shorter. The males wore loincloths or breeches; the females, linen robes. Most of them were adorned with bracelets and necklaces of feather, bone, metal and jewels. They stood in a semicircle around a large, polished disk of black stone. The distant stalactites reflected darkly in its surface.

"You're...you're elves." Johnny's voice was tinged with wonder.

"We're *tzapame*, and no doubt about that." Their guide seemed a little offended, but mostly amused. "Little People, older children of the Feathered One. We were here before humans, in other words."

Carol tried to smile, but hundreds of stony eyes regarded her, and she faltered. *The folk in the mountain. A stern, cold race.* "Did you…did you train my grandmother?"

"Train? Well, we sure did teach her a lot. Your mother, too. Though there's some as thinks that was a big mistake, all things considered. They call me Pingo. I am pretty much the youngest here. They chose me to guide you and to be their voice because I can speak English. Most of these older fellows have barely gotten used to Spanish. Many of them still think *Nahuatl* is too new-fangled. *Tzapame* live a horribly long time."

Johnny's hands clenched and unclenched with nervous energy. "Pingo, our mother disappeared six months ago. We…I thought she was dead. My father thought she left on purpose. Do you…can you…"

"Take it easy, son. You're getting ahead of me. First off, your ma ain't dead."

A wave of emotion hit Carol and her knees buckled. Two female *tzapame* stepped forward and grabbed her elbows before she fell. *She's alive. Thank God. Johnny was wrong.*

"She's been taken. Abducted by dark forces and dragged down to Mictlan, the Underworld."

What? Carol knew what Mictlan was, one of the possible destinations for the dead in the Aztec religion. Her mind boggled. *Wait. It's real? There's an actual Aztec Land of the Dead?*

Johnny seemed to just brush aside the impossibility of what

they were hearing. "But why? Why would anyone want to kidnap her?

Pingo lowered his eyes for a second, and then glanced back up, his expression somber. "Because of you two. Because of what you are."

Carol took a deep breath, steadying herself. "Shapeshifters? But so is she!"

"Not just shifters: *twin naguales*. Very special."

Shaking his head, Johnny grunted his disapproval. "Doesn't make sense. If these 'dark forces' wanted us, why not just kidnap us?"

Several of the *tzapame* began speaking simultaneously. Pingo nodded, gestured, and muttered quick replies.

"We don't rightly know. There are possibilities, but *there's no time*. You have to go after her. Now. He's had her too long already."

Carol's heart felt as if it might explode any moment. "Wait. You want us to travel *into...Hell* to rescue our mother? How are we supposed to do that?"

Pingo sneered. "First, it's *Mictlan*, not Hell. The Underworld. Place of shades. The dead go Beyond by many paths, each one different from the next; for the living, however, only the old roads will serve. But twin *naguales*...such must take the Black Road through the Nine Deadly Deserts."

Carol thought she might throw up.

"Okay," quipped Johnny. "That doesn't sound too good."

"You'll have help, I promise. There are many things we can offer you."

Several *tzapame* approached, bearing items in their slender hands. They gave each of them a strange leather amulet from which dangled feathers, animal teeth and bones.

"Johnny, your bracelet and Carol's necklace will help you get past most obstacles, once you master their use."

And who's going to teach us to use them? Carol didn't ask.

Another pair of Little People placed a clay jar in each of their hands. Water sloshed inside them and they were sealed with a wax plug. From a small handle on the side of each hung a leather thong.

"When the heat becomes unbearable and clouds of ash choke you, may this water provide some relief."

Two more *tzapame* strode forward.

"Now, open your mouths. If you don't mind."

This is insane, Carol thought, but she complied. The Little Person in front of her laid a piece of red jade on her tongue.

"I reckon this is a lot to ask, but please swallow the jade. It'll keep your hearts safe when all appears lost."

I give up. She swallowed the stone; Johnny did the same. Another of the *tzapame* drew near, bearing a little bag full of jewels.

"Okay, this is where I draw the line," Johnny exclaimed. "I am *not* going to swallow all those damn stones Pingo."

Pingo laughed. It was a harsh sound, but joyful all the same, and it reassured her. "Johnny, you don't have to eat these, partner. They're gifts for Mictlantecuhtli and Mictecacíhuatl, Lord and Lady of the Dead. When you reach the end of your journey, they're going to have their big bony hands outstretched for some goods. Give them the jewels, and they'll let you through."

Behind him, a group of *tzapame* had formed a ring around the

black disk. They began chanting in that ancient language Pingo
had used to access the chamber. A thrumming filled the cavern,
building so that it was soon vibrating Carol's bones. Smoke began
to ooze from the dark, mirror-like surface.

"Listen," Pingo said, coming closer to them. "There's not
much I can tell you. But know this: I'm not like the others. I was
once human, like you. I also lost my mother, but I never got her
back. There is no worse feeling in the universe, I promise you. It
almost tore me to bits. So you push ahead, no matter what. I know
you're thinking this is madness, that you're not prepared. None of
that matters. You have our gifts, and I pray they will serve you.
But the most important gift we cannot give you—it already lies
within you both."

The black disk groaned. Great gouts of smoke billowed into
the cavern, thick and foul. The thrumming began to shake the
walls and dust showered down on them.

"You have to pass through the *chay abah*, the sacred obsidian
mirror." Pingo's voice had become a shout. "Be wary of the river.
And look to the dog. He will scare the bejeezus out of you, but
you can trust him."

The *tzapame* herded them to the smoking mirror. Carol's soul
seemed to gibber with fear, but she remembered the glow of her
tonal, and she grimly set her teeth. Johnny looked at her and
stretched out his hand. She took it.

"At the end of things, remember who you are!" Pingo's face
contorted as he screamed to be heard above the ghastly howl of
the mirror. "And don't forget. *Look to the dog!*"

Then the twins stepped onto the mirror, and the world
shattered.

CHAPTER SIX

Reality was crumbling around them. Johnny couldn't see anything, but he felt and heard great chunks breaking away and sliding into the void. Instinctively, he knew that his own flesh would soon be in danger. Gripping his sister's hand more tightly, he moved forward. It was like pressing against a sheet of plastic, a membrane that gave slightly but wouldn't allow them through. Johnny was nothing if not stubborn, though. He strained with every ounce of will he possessed. The membrane stretched further and further. He could feel Carol shoving against it as well. Together they advanced through the howling dissolution till the barrier gave way and, with a sudden snapping sensation, they tumbled through.

Johnny rose to his feet, dusting himself off. Lifting his eyes, he took in the strange panorama. Behind him, stretching away in all directions, was a curtain of mist that seemed to curve slightly in the distance. The ground he stood on was covered with glittering black sand of apparently painfully rough texture, to judge from the way Carol sat cursing and picking bits of it out of her palms. Ahead of them, perhaps a hundred yards away, a river flowed darkly. *It's freaking huge*, Johnny thought. *Can't even see the other shore.*

"Johnny," Carol asked, rising to her feet at last, "where are the stars?"

Looking up, Johnny was surprised to find, not the overhanging rock of an enormous cavern, but an empty sky that glowed with gloomy grayness. There was no visible sun, moon or stars. From time to time strange black forms were silhouetted against the gloaming, too far away to distinguish clearly.

"Okay, this is officially freaking me out," he muttered. He turned back to the wall of mist. It stretched all the way up into the weird sky, blending into the gray expanse. Reaching out a hand, he probed the foggy barrier. It was resilient to the touch, pushing back at him. "I'm guessing this is the membrane we just came through."

"Listen," his sister whispered. From within the mist came unearthly sounds: deep roars, rattling hisses, insane chattering.

"Okay," Johnny breathed with forced humor. "Time to look for another way out of here. Maybe the river?"

Glancing about, Carol groaned. "There's nothing here. No trees, no rocks. Nothing. How are we supposed to cross it, swim?"

A low, growling voice chuckled. "I wouldn't recommend it, dear. You'd drown before you got to the other side."

Johnny turned and almost fainted. A huge dog was standing beside him, its massive head on a level with that of a tall man. Black lips curled back in a horrifying grin that revealed long, pointed teeth. The creature's blunt snout crinkled up as it smiled, and its blue eyes radiated human-like intelligence. Short pointed ears twitched as the twins took several steps back. Johnny saw that the left one was ragged, as if chewed on in a fight. The hellhound eased its wrinkled bulk back onto its haunches, perhaps trying to make them feel less threatened. Its short, reddish fur, Johnny noted, was crisscrossed with scars.

"Of course, drowning would be the least of your worries," it continued, its mouth impossibly forming English words. "There are all sorts of hideous beasts inhabiting the Chignahuapan. Trust me when I say that you would not want to face them alone."

Carol was the one who finally spoke, her voice trembling. "As opposed to facing them with...you?"

The dog cocked its head oddly. "Precisely. Didn't the *tzapame* tell you about me?"

Johnny cleared his throat. "Well, Pingo did mention a dog..."

The hellhound's eyes narrowed. "Pingo, eh? Leave it to that little fool to muddle such an essential bit of information. A quick introduction then. I am Xolotl. Let me say that slowly: show-*low*-tull. Master of Lightning, Lord of the West, Guardian of the Sun. A shapeshifter, somewhat like the two of you."

"Are you..." stammered Carol "...are you a god?"

Xolotl laughed, a low, pleasant rumble. "No, girl. Not a god. The *tonal* of a god, his beastly side. The part of him able to pad through the darkness and stop the slimy things that crave destruction. I've been sent to give you aid, to the degree that I can."

His heart still pounding in fear of the huge dog, Johnny took a tentative step forward. "Why?"

"Pardon me?"

"Why give us aid? I mean, we're here to get our mom back. I don't understand why some mysterious god's animal soul would be interested in that. Don't you guys have like more important stuff to worry about?"

Xolotl lowered its head to look more fully into Johnny's eyes. "Juan Ángel Garza, I assure you that there is presently nothing more important than this quest of yours. Though, hrm, I don't quite remember why."

"You don't," Johnny tried to sound as cold as possible, "*remember*? What the heck does that mean?"

"Come, boy. Tell me it's easy for you to recall your human life when you're in jaguar form. Some things are forgotten. That's the price we pay for this ability. What I do know is that you are both very special. Twin *naguales* are very rare, and very sought after. Different factions of extremely powerful beings will want to discover whether you possess *xoxal*."

"Show shawl? What's that?" Carol asked.

"Savage magic. A special sort of spiritual energy that, very infrequently, twin shapeshifters are able to wield. Being so rare, it is little understood. The ancients used to say that *xoxal* was the ultimate power to create or destroy, to heal or obliterate. Among other things this savage magic should allow you to transform into virtually any animal."

"Whoa. That would rock." Johnny imagined shifting into a cheetah. Or a bear.

Xolotl closed its eyes and gave a shudder. "I'm afraid it's been quite some time since I last visited the realm of men. It sounds as if you're speaking English, but I'm not always certain what you mean."

"He means that it would be great," Carol put in. Johnny snorted, half in irritation, half in amusement. His heart rate had returned to normal. The hellhound, though imposing, no longer made him want to run away in fear.

"So, how do we know if we've got, uh, *xoxal*?"

"Unfortunately, it has been centuries since the last pair of *xoxal*-gifted *naguales* walked the earth. They, hrm, lost their lives fighting a great evil, so their lore wasn't passed down to anyone else. Besides, I seem to recall that the power is different for each set of twins, so I don't know that it would be of particular use to know what previous *naguales* had done to trigger their abilities."

"Wow," Johnny muttered snarkily. "That's really helpful."

Xolotl regarded him intently and rose to all fours. *Oh, crap, now I've made him mad! I've got to stop being such a jerk all the time. Especially to huge freaking hellhounds.*

"I understand your confusion and desperation." The super-natural beast's features softened as if in compassion. "It is difficult to lose someone you love, to search for them in frightening places, and to have to find within yourself the strength to overcome obstacles that ought to destroy you. You have both shown great courage by simply coming this far. You've faced your true natures without falling to pieces. I admire that tenacity. Cling to your stubbornness—you will need it direly."

Johnny glanced at Carol pointedly. They both had a long history of being hard-headed, so no problem there.

"Pingo, I hope, explained that you travel by the Black Road. Very few souls leave the realm of men by this route any longer, and its guardians have grown restless and hungrier for cruelty than ever before. But if you are to rescue your mother and thereby stop the dark forces that even now rally against your world, you will have to face them. I will be your guide, so far as I can. What little I know, I will teach you. In the end, however, you two will face your mother's captor alone. To be victorious, you must be true to who you are."

Gah. More cryptic garbage. But a part of Johnny felt energized by Xolotl's words. He liked challenges, liked competing. *If I can do something, I can do it really well. Always have been able to. So I'll get this magic stuff down in time to kick some underworld butt. I'm sure of it.*

"Okay, then." Carol nodded, her lower lip trembling just a little. "So I'm guessing our first obstacle is getting around that ginormous river."

"Yes, Carolina. Luckily for you, no skill of yours is required this time around. All you need to do is to climb upon my back and grab a fold of skin. Don't worry about hurting me, you can't. Come on, now."

What the heck. Might as well. After securing his clay water jug to a belt loop with the leather thong, Johnny gripped Xolotl's skin and hauled himself up. The fur was surprisingly soft. Reaching his hand down to his sister, he laughed. "Better than riding a pony, Carol. I don't think you'll fall off this time."

Her face red, Carol ignored his hand and clambered up on her own. "Don't start with me, Johnny, or I'll tell Xolotl that you're not a dog person."

The hound's mirth rumbled beneath their legs. "This is good. Humor is good. Joy is better, but humor will do for now."

With a bound he set off. The water was dark, and Johnny figured that meant it was very deep. *This is no ordinary river. We're in Mictlan now. It might go on forever.*

As if reading his mind Xolotl growled a warning. "Don't let go of me, not for a second. There's no retrieving you if you fall. The depths of Chignahuapan are a dark corner of the universe that not even I dare explore."

"Do you always swim people across?"

"People, never. You're the only living humans to ever set foot in this place. I've ferried gods across, however, and a soul or two. The souls that once traveled this path to Beyond were buried with dogs, and the shades of those loyal beasts would bear their masters across. But those days are long past."

The hellhound plunged into the inky waters, its legs pedaling beneath them. The light currents tugged coldly at the twins' calves. Carol's teeth chattered. *Like mom, she can't stand the cold.* An image flashed through his mind: his mother, wrapped in a blanket, sitting at her worktable at 2am. The memory made his chest ache, but there was nothing much to distract him. Above them the gray sky stretched on forever, and on all sides the black waters steadily flowed. The twins and their guide advanced quickly, but the river seemed endless. That got Johnny thinking about the geography of the Underworld.

"So, Xolotl. What would've happened if we had, I don't know, decided not to cross the river? If we just started walking along that black sand?"

"You would eventually circle back to where you started. Several years from now."

"What about crossing back through the, uh, curtain?"

"You would be as lost as if you had tied a stone round your neck and dropped into the river. Like most hells, Mictlan is circular. The only way out is to head toward the center."

Carol shivered violently. "Wait, 'most hells'? You mean there's more than one?"

"Yes, Carolina. But let's focus on this one, shall we?"

What felt like hours passed in relative silence, empty except for the splashing of water and Carol's steady breathing. But the quiet wasn't so bad. It was the sitting still that was driving Johnny crazy. He hated having nothing to do. *Like Mom,* he mused. *We both have to be active or we get antsy. Dad used to say we suffered from ADHD.*

He was about to make some sort of clever quip when something grabbed his foot and *pulled.*

"Uh, Xolotl? There's something under..."

It came again. This time, Johnny almost lost his balance. Carol twisted around, her eyes wide. "Put your arms around my waist!"

"What? No! I've got a good..."

A violent tug pulled his sneaker from his left foot.

"What the...Something just stole my damn tennis shoe!"

"Johnny, put your arms around me, now!"

An old anger rushed up within him. "Don't tell me what to do, Carol. You're not my mom. You're not older than me. I don't have to listen to..."

Now he felt the slimy thing curl around his foot, tightening like a noose. He tried to kick himself free.

"Crap! It's got me!"

"*¡Juan Ángel Garza,*" Carol shouted, "*que me abraces ya!*"

Grumbling but afraid, he did as Carol said, conditioned by years of his mother's shouted commands in Spanish. She leaned forward and wrapped her own arms tightly about Xolotl's neck. "Uh, if it's not too much to ask, could you *swim faster, please*?"

Snarling at some bone-white coils that broke the water beside them, the hellhound began to churn the water in earnest. The grip on Johnny's foot was nearly unbearable.

"It won't let go!"

One of the milky tentacles came closer, and Xolotl snapped its jaws on the creature, shaking it mercilessly. Johnny's foot was released.

"Okay, I'm okay!"

Xolotl, perhaps drawing on deep reserves of energy, began to rocket across the water. The far shoreline was now visible, a broken horizon of jagged rock. After a few minutes of sustained speed, the hellhound slowed. Carol's death grip on the beast's neck slackened, and Johnny sat up straighter, seizing a fold of Xolotl's skin as he let go of his sister.

"I believe the danger has passed." The hellhound turned its head and examined them with one wise blue eye.

"Leaving me with just one shoe," Johnny muttered.

"You'll not be needing shoes, for the most part."

"Uh, do you see all those sharp rocks over there? You planning to let me ride your back all the way to the Lord and Lady of the Dead or whatever?"

Xolotl sighed heavily, causing the twins to shift. "You're *naguales*. Your journey will largely be made in animal form."

"But we can't even control it!"

"You'll have to learn."

Carol turned and looked at him. Her eyes were full of tears. "You have trust me, Johnny. If I tell you to do something, you've got to just do it."

"What?" *Drama queen. Like always.*

"You could have *died*! That thing might've pulled you into the river, and you'd sink and keep on sinking, and what would I do then, huh?"

She turned her back on him, stifling a sob.

The long silence that followed was suddenly interrupted by Xolotl's rumbling, growly voice. "After that attack, you're probably wondering why such a place as this even exists. What sort of a god would put souls through such torture just to move Beyond?"

Several snide comments ran through Johnny's mind, but he kept his mouth shut and listened.

"From the very beginning, the oldest gods appointed a pair of brothers to oversee the development of life on your world, to ensure the balance of growth and decay, creation and destruction, life and death. Twins. They've had many names, but the Aztecs called them Quetzalcoatl and Tezcatlipoca. Well, as is sadly often the case, one brother's envy of the other destroyed their friendship. Tezcatlipoca, hating the joy that creation brought Quetzalcoatl, began to undermine or outright destroy those creations, upsetting the balance. Time and again he wiped out life on earth. Quetzalcoatl, undaunted, would simply begin again.

"Finally, human beings came into existence and Tezcatlipoca, for some reason, decided to twist humanity to his purposes instead of obliterating it. One of the tools he used was fear, especially fear of death. But humans needed something tangible to fear, so the Lord of Chaos went to his brother the Lord of Creation and proposed a deal: he would not destroy man as long as he could create a way station for their souls, a stopover on their journey beyond all gods' reach. Quetzalcoatl agreed, because he believed people's faith and hope would be more powerful than their fear of the Underworld and its trials."

Johnny leaned back a little, reflecting on the strange story. *Is that why there's evil in the world? Because one brother is crazy jealous of his twin?*

Carol cleared her throat and reached up to rub Xolotl between the ears. "You're his *tonal*, aren't you? Quetzalcoatl's."

The hellhound said nothing for the space of several seconds, then murmured, "Yes."

She doesn't get it, though. She's all relieved and teary-eyed. But if Xolotl, Quetzalcoatl's animal self, is helping us, then that probably means Tezca-whatever has got mom. Which means we're stuck in the middle of the oldest family feud in the universe.

Wonderful.

CHAPTER SEVEN

I'm pretty sure Johnny doesn't get it. Xolotl is trying to warn us about what will happen if we can't trust each other. The menso nearly slipped into the depths because of the chip on his shoulder. Why can't he just understand that I would never do anything to hurt him? That my advice is for his good?

As Xolotl crossed the final few kilometers to the inner shore of the river, Carol contemplated ways of broaching the subject with her brother without making him mad. He had their mother's explosive personality, her tendency to make snap judgments and rush to conclusions without all the evidence. Most of the time, because of how insightful and perceptive the two of them were, those conclusions were correct, which made it even harder to convince them to slow down and review the evidence.

Carol and her dad, on the other hand, took their time when making decisions. Perhaps they even took too much time. They listened carefully to other points of view, read all sorts of material about a subject before slowly synthesizing a response. Carol understood, of course, that there were situations in which time just didn't permit that sort of thoroughness. *And that's why we were such a good team. Our family balanced itself. If Johnny and I are going get mom back, we're going to have to find that balance again.*

Before she knew it, they had made it across. Xolotl's broad paws stepped carefully onto the shattered gray stones that lined the river bank. After a few minutes, they found themselves on a sandy plain on which strange, stunted trees twisted like palsied hands. Before them lay low, rocky hills that built gradually toward a steep mountain range whose slopes glittered blackly in the eternal gloom.

"Obsidian." Johnny muttered, slipping from Xolotl's back. He stood on one leg, pulling off his other sneaker. His white socks contrasted starkly with the slate-colored sand. "That is just freaking great. We've got to scale mountains of sharp volcanic rock, and I'm in my stupid *socks*."

"Well," Carol said, trying to follow Xolotl's advice and inject a little humor, "the Hobbits crossed Mordor in their bare feet, so you've got to keep perspective, no?"

"*¿Qué?* Did Carolina Garza just make a funny?" Johnny rolled his eyes, but smiled.

"Excuse me, but...what is a, 'Hobbit'?"

Carol dropped to the ground and patted the hellhound reassuringly. "Literary allusion. A sort of big-footed elf."

"Dude, that's sacrilege! Hobbits are not elves!"

She waved him away dismissively. "Whatever. You never even read the books, Johnny. Just watched the movies obsessively." She leaned toward Xolotl. "You know what movies are, right?"

"Certainly. I visited several nickelodeons in San Francisco and Los Angeles before I left the realm of men."

"Huh?" The only nickelodeon Carol knew was the cable station.

"Whoa, that was a long time ago," Johnny muttered. To Carol he added smugly, "Nickelodeons were the first movie theaters, way back in the early 1900s."

"Thanks for the heads-up." She gave an exaggerated sigh, but was inwardly happy. *We can still josh around. Good sign.* "But, yeah, going back to your footwear problem…"

Xolotl walked away from them and shook himself vigorously, sending a spray of cold water in all directions. "I keep telling you," he growled once he was dry enough to stop, "that you don't need shoes. You need to learn how to shift. You won't make it through the Nine Deadly Deserts otherwise."

"But the truth is," Carol insisted, "that we can't control the transformations. I mean, the last time I was sort of half aware of what was going on. I was asleep, and then I felt this pressure build up inside of me, and I just, you know, *let go*, let it remake me. I was able to sense through my *tonal* and stuff, but I wasn't the one that caused it to happen, you see?"

Xolotl nodded his enormous head. "Of course I see. What you are failing to realize is that your animal self is *always* there, waiting, anxious to step forward. There's not much you have to do to convince it. Simply look for it, just beneath the surface of your conscious mind, and call to it. It will respond eagerly, I assure you."

The hellhound looked at her with an expectant gaze. When she did nothing, he scuffed his right front paw against the sand.

"What…now? You want me to try to transform *here*?"

"No time like the present, Carolina. You, too, Juan Ángel."

Carol closed her eyes, attempting to focus, searching for that glowing, vital, hungry part of herself. But her mind kept snapping back to their predicament, to her concern about her mother, to her confusion about the trials ahead.

Gritting her teeth in frustration, she groaned and stomped her foot. "Gah! I can't do it. I can't focus."

"It isn't about focus, girl, but about a lack thereof."

Carol glanced at Johnny, whose face was twisted up so comically that she almost laughed despite herself. After a few more seconds, he muttered a curse and opened his eyes. "Forget it. I got nothing."

Xolotl bared his teeth in a feral gesture. "What you need is to confront the perils of this place head-on. That'll knock you free of your comfortable mindsets." He sounded positively angry. Carol was rather taken aback. "The danger you're in, that your mother is in, that we are *all of us* in, hasn't really penetrated your barely adolescent brains. You act as if this were a game. You've never had to face a real trial in your lives. You're complacent."

"What the hell are you talking about?" Johnny was livid. "Complacent? No trials? What do you think we've been living the last six months, huh? Not knowing where our mom is, watching our dad get drunker and drunker every day...you're not being fair, man."

"Fair? Johnny, fairness is irrelevant. If you can't transform, *you can't save your mother*. If you think I'm being unduly harsh, I suggest you imagine her dying in the dark, all alone, because you couldn't free yourself from your own self-control."

They stood in silence, regarding one another. *So much for humor and joy, huh?*

"Well, come on," the hellhound said finally. "Let's begin. First you will cross this range, the *Tepeme Monamictia* or Crashing

Mountains. Then come the deserts: blackness, bats and jaguars, cold, haunted ruins, lava plains, ashes, heart-eating demons, obsidian winds and a putrid lake. Then you stand before the Lord and Lady of Death, and once past them you *finally* confront the villain who holds your mother prisoner. The *tzapame* have given you some tools; I am providing you some assistance. But in the end it is the two of you who must rise to the challenges and overcome the obstacles.

"Words of warning: you will neither feel hunger or sleepiness. You may nonetheless be tempted to eat or sleep. Do *not*. Even though you will become physically very tired, you cannot afford to rest much. The time is short. Your enemies know you are here. Move quickly and face them with courage."

He began to lope toward the hills. The twins exchanged a look and dashed after him. At first they kept a decent pace, crossing the sandy plane with flying strides. At the hills they slowed somewhat, bounding from rock to rock, avoiding fissures and scree. As the hills began to become the roots of the obsidian-rich mountains, their path grew steeper, and they had to use their hands more and more, nicking themselves occasionally on sharp points and edges. Carol heard more and more muttered curses coming from her brother, so she looked down at his feet. His socks were stained red with blood.

"Stop!" she ordered. "Johnny, your feet! My God...Xolotl, look at his feet!"

The hellhound gave a low snarl. "I told you what you needed to do. That you refuse to comply is another matter entirely."

Johnny sat down heavily on the flinty slope and examined the soles of his feet. "This sucks, big time." He closed his eyes, lay back, and folded his arms across his chest.

"What are you doing?" Xolotl demanded.

"Going to sleep, man. That's the only way I know to shift."

"I've told you, you can't sleep in Mictlan, child."

Johnny's eyes shot open. "You know, I'm getting real tired of your freaking attitude. I mean, yeah, you're the shadow soul of Quetzalcoatl or whatever, and you helped us cross the humongous river, but could you just back the heck off?"

Xolotl's blue eyes seemed to glow like burning alcohol. "I see that what you require are very drastic measures."

The hellhound reared up on his hind legs. *Oh, crap*, thought Carol. *He's going to attack Johnny to force a transformation.*

But instead, Xolotl began to quiver and shrink, fingers emerging from the tips of his ever-smaller paws, his snout pulling back into his face, red hair falling about him like autumn pine needles. Within seconds a man stood before them. He had medium-length blond hair sweeping back from his lined forehead and blue eyes surrounded by a network of fine wrinkles and scars. Wrapped around him was a red-furred animal skin that covered most of his sun-toasted flesh.

"Let's see how long you manage without my guidance," he said in a cultured, old-fashioned voice. Spinning curtly on his heel, he stepped behind an outcropping and was gone from sight. Carol followed, but there was nothing. He had disappeared without a trace.

"Fantastic. He vanished."

"Figures. Whatever. Who needs him? Here, give me a hand."

Carol helped her brother to his feet. Wincing, he leaned on her and together they made their way up the winding, steep path that the passage of a million souls had only faintly carved into the obsidian mountain. Soon Johnny was leaving bloody footprints behind.

This is insane. You'd think that the Lord of Creation or whatever would have enough compassion to help us out. We're twelve years old, Quetzalcoatl, in case you'd forgotten. Cut us some slack, okay?

Johnny had begun to whimper softly when they finally reached the top. A flat defile stretched before them, wide enough for three people to walk abreast, lined by glittering crags that loomed darkly above. A stiff, moaning wind blew toward them from beyond the passage. Thousands of years of erosion had worn the floor smooth and level, and a smile of relief spread across Johnny's face as he took his first few steps.

"Oh, man, that feels good. Nice and cool, too. Like the Saltillo tile at home when mom mops. Mopped. You know what I mean."

Carol nodded and rubbed her brother's back. "Well, according to 'Clifford the Big Red Dog' the deserts start just beyond this. What did he say the first one was? Blackness, right? Doesn't sound too bad."

They walked another ten meters when a horrible crashing sound made them draw up short.

"What the..." Johnny began. They walked a few more paces, and the sound came again, accompanied by a tremor beneath their feet. Johnny gingerly extended one reddened sock and CRASH!

They stood still for several minutes. There were no more explosions or tremors, so they started ambling down the defile. They'd crossed some fifteen meters of passage that curved gradually toward the left when, without warning, the crags on either side not four yards ahead slammed into each other with a deafening smash and a hail of splintered rock and obsidian dust, then pulled back to their original positions.

"¡Hijo de su Pink Floyd!" Johnny screamed, using one of their mother's favorite nonsense curses. "Dude! If we had been standing there..."

Carol's heart pounded mercilessly. "Oh, Xolotl, you jerk. You couldn't have mentioned the dangerous smashing rocks?"

As if in answer, the walls a little further ahead slammed into each other. Carol gripped her brother's forearm.

"Johnny, I think that..."

SLAM! Less than half a meter *behind* them, the crags collided, coating them both in fine black dust and leaving their ears ringing.

"Oh, my God, Johnny! We're going to be killed!"

There was a weird expression on her brother's face. He was counting on his fingers and mumbling to himself.

"What? What are you doing, Johnny?" Her voice was strained by panic.

"Hang on, Carol. Relax a second. It's like...it's like a video game."

"Huh?"

"Yeah. There's a pattern. You figure it out, and you can get through. One crash, followed a minute later by another and then one more just a few seconds after that. Then something like four minutes passes and the pattern starts again."

Carol suddenly understood. "Which means..."

"Which means we have less than three minutes, dude, so RUN!"

CHAPTER EIGHT

ohnny's feet pounded the slick rock, every step sending shudders of pain along his legs. *Next crash could happen anywhere. Got to keep moving.* The blood on the soles of his feet made him slip every few yards, and he was certain that at any second he would end up on his back, the crags slamming into him. But then the last explosive collision came from far behind them, and he slowed his pace, putting a hand on Carol's shoulder to let her know the danger had passed.

Breathing heavily, the twins emerged from the passage on the other side of the mountain. A smoother, more gradual slope greeted them, promising an easier descent down into a valley shrouded in thick mist. Leaning against a boulder, Johnny took a rest.

"Looks like regular granite and sand on this side," he mused, rubbing a hand against a rock. "Which is, you know, impossible in the real world. I guess this...place? Dimension? Gah, this Underworld has different laws of physics and stuff. But it should be easier on my feet."

"What you need is something to bind them up." Carol looked herself up and down. "But we're just wearing jeans and t-shirts, so there's not much material to use."

Johnny nodded. "Yeah. This is one of those times when I

wish I listened to Dad. He's always bugging me to wear a belt, like it makes me more of a man or something dumb like that."

The image of their father that came to him wasn't of the present drunken, broken man, but of Dr. Oscar Garza, decked out in his suit and tie, hair a little unruly, a book tucked under one arm, a cheesy joke on his lips. The memory was poignant, almost painful. Johnny realized with a start that he didn't just miss his mother. He missed the man his father used to be, the man he admired despite their differences. His eyes burned with the realization.

"Maybe we'll find something down at the bottom," Carol mused. "We could tie wood to the bottoms of your feet with my shoelaces. You really shouldn't have thrown away your other shoe, Johnny. We could've..."

Before she could finish with her irritating scolding, the slope in front of them exploded into the air in a geyser of sand and rock. Towering above them, its body coiling free from the ground, a massive white serpent hissed loudly and opened wide its dark red mouth. Two enormous fangs, each the length of one of Johnny's legs, glinted bone-white and deadly in the gloom.

"Run!" Johnny screamed, shoving his sister ahead of him. They went stumbling down the side of the mountain as the serpent twisted around and dove, headfirst, after them. The ground shuddered violently beneath its weight. Risking a glance back, Johnny saw the infernal reptile slithering toward them, shoving boulders out of the way effortlessly, sending them flying into the air or tumbling in the direction of the fleeing twins. Pain was a distant memory. The journey's objective was forgotten. All that existed was the ineluctable danger behind and the boy racing to survive. In that purely instinctual drive for self-preservation, Johnny felt his *tonal* scratch at the edges of his mind, and with a sigh of relief, the boy stepped aside.

With a thrusting twist of magic, his animal soul reshaped his flesh, and his clothes fell away as the jaguar dug ebony claws into the gravel and wheeled about the face the giant snake. The white reptile shot past him, continuing its pursuit of the girl. The jaguar roared in anger and leapt onto the slick, cold skin, snapping his jaws and clawing viciously. Enraged and confused, the serpent curled back with a snap, its tail whipping about and sending the human girl sprawling in the sand. The jaguar clung tightly and sank his teeth into the snake, its strange, cold black blood squirting into his mouth. Hissing hoarsely with pain, the serpent tried to shrug the jaguar off, but coiled back around when it found its struggle useless. Opening its jaws impossibly wide, it flung its diamond-shaped head toward the girl, who had just rolled over and was regarding the demon rushing at her with wide, frightened eyes that closed for a moment before the wolf snarled its way to the surface of her being and scrabbled out of reach.

Johnny came forward a little, bonding with his *tonal* so that he could guide it with his conscious, human mind. He roared at Carol, who had run down the slope in her lupine form, the strange *tzapame* necklace still snug around her neck. She looked back and saw him struggling to hang on to the massive serpent. With a short, barking howl, she turned around and ran at the hellish reptile, leaping at the soft flesh below its head. Realizing that his sister had found the beast's weak spot, Johnny used his claws to clamber up its side. Together they ripped at the snake with their deadly teeth until great gouts of black began to squirt all over. They dropped to the ground and backed away, their hackles raised. The snake quivered for a moment and then fell, thudding like a dead weight against the mountainside.

After a few moments of staring at the twitching corpse of their enemy, Carol walked over to her clothes, nuzzling them into a pile that she picked up with her narrow snout. She ducked behind a boulder, and soon Johnny heard her speak.

"You should probably shift back and get dressed, Johnny. I don't particularly feel like seeing your naked butt walking around through Mictlan."

And how am I supposed to do that? Johnny was stumped for a second, staring down at his paws, at the mysterious bracelet that encircled his left foreleg, but then he realized that all he needed to do was to *come forward*, totally inhabiting his body. The tonal obediently backed off, and his body stretched and snapped itself back into the form of a twelve-year-old. To his delight, his feet were completely healed. He pulled on nearly all his clothes, abandoning only the bloody socks, which he was covering with a medium-sized rock when Carol emerged from behind the boulder.

"Wow." There was a look of wonderment on her face.

"I know, right? I guess it's good Xolotl's not around. He'd be all 'see, I told you it would be remarkably easy' and stuff. I really don't want to be chewed out right now."

Carol giggled. "Yeah, we're kind of *all chewed out*, huh?"

That cracked Johnny up. He doubled up with more laughter than her cheesy joke deserved, partly because it was nice to see her loosen up, partly because he had been so on edge that he needed the release. "That was pretty good," he managed to say after a few seconds. "All chewed out. Heh. Funny Carol."

He showed her his feet, and she gave him a hug for the first time in months. *Feels good to click again, like we used to. Nothing like killing a demon snake to bring a family together, I guess!*

They continued down the slope, laughing and comparing their impressions of the fight, what each had sensed in their *nagual* forms about the reptilian titan and the strange new landscape. They had both noticed the absence of the living web they had discovered they could perceive in their own world. "It's probably because, uh, yeah, this is the Land of the Dead," Carol ventured.

"Well, hello, but not even that snake seemed alive. Did you notice it had no scent? And what the heck was that black stuff? That sure wasn't blood. Didn't taste like a regular lizard or snake...and my *tonal* has eaten a bunch of those."

"Maybe it's some sort of demon, made out of weird, I don't know, supernatural stuff. And, Johnny? Lizards? Really? Gross."

"Uh, didn't you snack on a *tlachuache*?" He made a face and feigned a stuck-up fresa accent. "*Guácala. O sea, qué asco, en serio.*"

Carol sputtered with laughter. "Yeah, I guess an opossum is about on level with a...*Holy Mother of God!*"

"Huh?" Johnny looked up, and towering above them was a gigantic lizard, something like a cross between an alligator and a komodo dragon, its eyes yellow and malevolent, its many rows of teeth sharp, crooked and dripping with poisonous saliva that sent waves of fetid odors pouring over the twins.

"You," the reptile declared, its voice booming like the raging flames that destroy forests, homes and families, "have slain my brother Chalmecatl! Living intruders prepare to meet your doom in the jaws of Xochitonal!"

As it opened wide its maw, a shape came bounding down the mountain, hurtling at Xochitonal. It was the hellhound, Xolotl. They came together with an earthshaking thud, their forelegs wrapping around each other as they struggled, jaws reaching for each other's throats.

"Dude," Johnny muttered reverently, "it's like Godzilla versus King Kong or something!"

Xolotl flipped the great lizard onto its back, turning briefly toward the twins. "What are the two of you waiting for? I can only hold this creature off for so long! He can't follow you into the first desert..." the *tonal* of Quetzalcoatl leapt onto the reptile's belly "...so get yourselves down this mountain as fast as you can!"

Without waiting to see how the epic battle turned out, the twins began running down the remaining stretch of dark gray granite sand that lined the narrow confines of the Black Road. From behind them came apocalyptic sounds of struggle and destruction, but Johnny focused on the dark fog rising before them from the valley at the foot of the mountain. It seethed and swirled ominously, like virulent smoke from a witch's cauldron.

Blackness, he mused. *That's okay. I'm not afraid of the dark.*

They reached the bottom. Carol grabbed his hand, and together they plunged into the roiling mists.

CHAPTER NINE

They stepped into the dense fog and were immediately blinded. It was the most absolute darkness Carol had ever experienced, and it surrounded her. She lifted her free hand in front of her face. Nothing. She brought it closer, and closer, till her palm touched her nose. *Nothing.*

Johnny's grip on her hand tightened. "Carol." His whisper was deafening in the absolute silence that surrounded them. "I can't see a thing."

"Me neither. Don't let go. It would be so easy to get separated in this place."

They walked slowly forward, a few cautious steps at a time. The silence was overwhelming. Carol wanted to talk to her brother, hear his voice, wince at his stupid jokes and awkward laughter. But the darkness was too absolute. And, it seemed to grow, creeping into her mind.

Suddenly the black mist cleared, and she was looking...up the slope of the mountain they had just descended. The snarls and thuds that reached her ears, providing an ironic relief, indicated that Xolotl and the massive reptilian demon were still fighting.

"*Ah, que la...*" Johnny spat. "We walked in a damn circle! Come on, let's turn back around."

Carol quailed at the idea of re-entering that dark stillness. She suspected, not that something horrible awaited her within, but that the pitchy quiet itself would do something to her. *How long did Dad say souls took to cross Mictlan? Four years, I think. Xolotl keeps pushing us to hurry, but what if we get stuck wandering in circles in this mist for days? Weeks? Months? Is he going to come guide us out? Probably not.*

As Johnny pulled her into the desert again, she decided against sharing too many of her doubts with her twin. Instead, she tugged on his hand till he stopped.

"I think we should shift. Our *tonales* can probably navigate this place better than our human senses. Mom needs us. We can't afford to waste time."

"Okay. You're probably right. What about our clothes?"

"Take them off, stuff your shirt and underwear into your pants pockets, and tie the legs around your waist or neck. When you shift, the bundle should stay with you like your bracelet does."

Johnny cleared his throat a little awkwardly. "Yeah, okay. But we really need to get Big Red to teach us how to keep the animal skin after shifting back, like he did. That'd sure make life easier. Okay, I'm letting go of your hand. Don't wander off or anything. It's not like I can see you in this mess."

Carol nodded foolishly. *Hello, he just said he can't see me.* "Got it."

When he let go she felt completely unmoored in the darkness. Not even a single star for company. Utterly alone, filling up with silence.

"Hey, I'm right here." Johnny's voice was tinged with concern.

"Huh?"

"Your breathing got shallow and fast, like you were panicking. I haven't forgotten your fear of the dark, Dude. Don't worry. We're going to be alright."

"Okay. Thanks." Slipping out of her sneakers, Carol pulled off her t-shirt and jeans, shoving the thin white cotton into a pocket. Her sports bra and panties were next, leaving her feeling somewhat silly but mostly vulnerable, standing naked in the dark. Shoving her socks into her shoes, she strung them from belt loops beside the small clay water bottle, and she tied her jeans around her waist.

"Okay, I'm going to shift now. Don't go anywhere yet. We don't know how our senses are going to react to this mist."

"Got it." Johnny's voice cracked. *He's probably trying to shift already.* As she released control of herself to the hungry energy within her, her body writhed and was remade, bringing a whole new set of senses online. She could feel the faint thudding from the mountain behind her, a slight vibration beneath her paws. She could smell the jaguar not a meter away and hear his easy breathing clearly. And though she still could not see, a strange magnetic pull tingled in her mind. *North. I can sense which way is north when I'm shifted. But if this place is circular...North must mean toward the center. Good. We won't get turned around this time.*

With a short bark of warning, she began to lope in that direction. Beside her, Johnny's heavy paws padded soft on the granite sand. His breath moved nearly imperceptibly in and out of powerful feline lungs. And all around them, thick and unyielding, was the silent dark. The jaguar's faint noises faded gradually, the hypnotic rhythm of his gait becoming part of the stillness, the

DAVID BOWLES

absence in which a sound rumbled.

No. I know there is no sound in the silence. I was just a silly, sick little girl back then. There was no gurgling, creaky voice.

But there it was, all the same. A droning, low and constant. She tried to focus on something else, the texture of the sand, the tapping of her shoes and water jug against her ribs, the feel of her lupine teeth as her tongue draped across them. The silence crowded against her senses all the same, oozing its way inside, filling her mind with nothingness. Every fear was amplified. Every bit of self-doubt a reality.

It was the same as that summer five years ago. She and her brother were seven years old, and it was the first time they'd been apart for more than a day. Uncle Nando had taken Johnny on a fishing trip with him and his two sons. Carol had felt a little under the weather, and even if she'd been perfectly healthy, she probably wouldn't have wanted to spend the weekend in a tent in that south Texas heat.

The first night she had been unable to sleep. She was drawn to the night, like her mother, enjoying late hours. But this was different. It was genuine insomnia, made worse by the fever that was sinking its claws into her bones. She had slipped into the living room to watch TV quietly, but at 2am the parental controls had kicked in and turned their cable off. Carol had sat quivering in the dark, of which she was deathly afraid, and then she had begun to hear in the vast silence of their rural home the thrumming whisper of despair.

She hadn't slept at all that night.

Her mom had taken her across the border the next day, to their doctor in Progreso. The long wait, heat, and medicine had

78

kept her from taking a nap. She'd managed to sleep a couple of hours in the evening, but by midnight her eyes had been wide open. And that sound, that impossible sound, had grown audible again as she sat there in the dark, its oscillations getting sharper and sharper till they had felt like hammer blows. Leaping to her feet, wild with fear, she had run down the hallway to her parents' bedroom and thrown herself on their bed.

"What is it, Sweetie?" her father had groggily asked as she'd snuggled trembling into his shoulder.

"It's...it's the silence, *papi*."

"The silence? What do you mean?"

She had swallowed hard, understanding even at the age of seven how crazy she was going to sound. "There's a sound. In the silence. It...it wants to eat me up, I think."

Her father had sat up and placed his palms against her cheeks. "Oh, God, you're burning up with fever, Carolina. Stay here. Let me get some medicine." He'd brought her liquid analgesic and electrolyte water and placed a cool rag across her forehead. As he'd lain beside her, cradling her shaking body in his left arm, she'd felt safer, but still menaced. Her whimpering voice must have stirred something in Dr. Garza, because he had begun to hum a melody which had gradually become a strange, soft hymn:

> A song I sing to Tonantzin
> Asking her for guidance.
> I sing for hope, I sing for joy
> And drown out the silence.

She'd been lulled into a deep sleep by his gentle crooning,

and when she'd awakened nearly twenty-four hours later, her fever had disappeared. As had the thrum of the silence. Her doctor had explained about vibrations in the skull caused by this and that, but she had been sure that there was something... supernatural about her experience.

Now, surrounded by interminable swaths of dark stillness, she was under attack again. *An attack. That's just what it is. This is the first trial. Whoever has Mom knows my weaknesses. He's trying to break me...isn't he?*

All about her, the silence seemed to swell, blotting out even the muted, rhythmic padding and breathing of her brother. She slipped further and further down into herself, trying to escape. Her *tonal*, unbridled and exulted, began to run as the silence chased her into the depths of her being, relentlessly drowning all contact with anything other than her own fears and inadequacies.

Alone in the existential dark, she was like a flame, guttering in a quiet gale.

And in that absolute loneliness, that darkness and that drowning, she realized she was not alone.

A voice, full of love and tenderness, whispered one word:

Sing.

From within her, past all her foibles and fears, the words came flowing like a crystal stream, noisy and joyous and pure.

> *A song I sing to Tonantzin*
> *Asking her for guidance.*
> *I sing for hope, I sing for joy*
> *And drown out the silence.*
> *The Little People in a ring,*

The sky begins to brighten:
They dance and chant before the dawn
And drown out the silence.

With mighty guards the sun comes up
And shines on the horizon:
The warriors loose a victory cry
And drown out the silence.

The quetzal and the mockingbird,
The dog and mountain lion,
Their voices join in raucous praise
And drown out the silence.

With every verse, she pushed back against the suffocating stillness until she had thrust it completely out of her. She reined in her tonal and slowed her pace, broadcasting her song into the dark, fighting back against her unseen enemy. Soon her perception was clear, but there was no one to perceive.

Johnny was gone.

It's my tonal. *Without ties to my human soul, it became a pure wolf. Wolves and jaguars...yeah, no. Not normally allies. The wolf ran away from Johnny. As far away as it could.*

Lifting her head, she scented the cold, still air. She couldn't sense him nearby. She opened her muzzle and howled loudly, but the mist muted and distorted her call. Johnny wouldn't be able to find her. He might even get turned around and wander, lost, searching for her.

I'm not giving up, do you hear me? She sent her thought like her song into the dark. *You're not going to win that easy, whatever the hell you are.*

The silence around her seemed to thicken in response. Then it curdled. She pictured some horrible creature smiling at her mockingly.

Wait. If I was able to use my song to defend myself...

Tensing herself inwardly, she tapped the inner well of music and bent the melody into a name.

Johnny!

Johnny! Come find your sister!

Johnny! Johnny! She's waiting in the dark!

Pouring every ounce of her love for the annoying boy into the words, she called again and again. Like a faint echo in her mind, she finally heard a response.

Carol? Are you singing?

Come on, Johnny! Come and find your sister!

Dude, what the heck? Either I'm going nuts, or you're talking into my brain!

Allowing the song to slide into the background, Carol tried just projecting her thoughts. *More like into your soul. I think I found my* xoxal, *Johnny. The savage magic. Can you track my thoughts?*

Yeah, they're getting louder, like I'm getting closer or something. Where did you go? Why did you just run off like that? I thought for sure I'd lost you. I was pretty mad.

That was just my tonal, acting on its own.

And where were you, then?

Something was attacking the conscious side of me, my human soul or whatever.

What? What do you mean?

Okay. You remember when I was sick? Five years ago?

Oh, yeah. You freaked out about the dark and how quiet it was.

Mom thought you might be schizophrenic or something.

Well, it wasn't my imagination, Johnny. Whatever has Mom, that's the thing that tried to eat up my mind when I was little. And it came after me, again. Its power is like...formed out of darkness and silence. It uses it to draw on your deepest fears and to make you feel so alone that you...give up.

A feeling of understanding entered Carol, flowing from her brother. Apparently emotions as well as words could be shared through the *xoxal* link. *Dude,* Johnny thought at her, *that means...that means they've been after us for a while. Whoa. We must be really valuable. I thought Big Red was just yanking our chain. Heh. That's funny. Get it? Chain? Dog?*

Carol sent a wave of love and joy at her goofy brother. Even his stupid jokes were a delight when compared to that dark, still, emptiness.

Wow. What was that? It felt like the nicest hug in the universe. Thanks, sis.

His voice was clear and loud and bright in her mind, the utter opposite of their enemy's quiet black magic. With great happiness she distinguished the vaguely unpleasant feline odor his animal form gave off and heard his labored breathing as he rushed to nuzzle her.

I think we're about through this first desert, he thought. *Can you see the glimmerings of light ahead?*

Carol's keen nocturnal eyes pierced the darkness and made out the contours of the mist, swirling against gray light just ahead. *Yeah, I see them. Race you out of this freaking place?*

You're on!

They sped out of the darkness, together.

CHAPTER TEN

They emerged onto a vast expanse of rolling dunes. Johnny slowed and stopped, his pupils dilating painfully even at the muted light from the gray sky above. The dunes were dotted with brown, stunted, thorny shrubs and dead trees. And spread everywhere, in glaring contrast with the dark granite sand, were millions and millions of bones.

Yikes. He looked over at his sister. *Okay, I'm going behind that big dead tree over there to shift and get dressed.*

Good idea. She loped toward another.

A few minutes later, they stood side by side, staring out at the enormous bone-strewn wilderness. Johnny scratched his head and squinted, trying to make out what lay beyond the horizon.

"So, let's see," Carol said. "What was next? Bats and jaguars. Gah."

Johnny shrugged. "Can't be all that bad. I mean, we can just bite the bats' heads off. As for jaguars...I can probably communicate with them or something. Worst case scenario, we just run like mad to the next desert."

"I don't know. Let's hope so." His sister stretched, her joints popping. The transition to human form tended to leave them a little sore. "I just think that the trials are going to keep getting harder. Dad said that they were meant to strip all earthly connections away from the souls of the deceased. I'm pretty sure that means they are *crazy* hard to get past."

Carol's negativity could be a little frustrating. "Yeah, but we're not dead. Plus, we're *naguales*. Different skill set, don't you think?"

"Sure, you're probably right."

Slapping his hands together like their mom always did before beginning a particularly difficult project, Johnny nodded. "Okay, then, let's get going."

They drudged up and down several dunes, sometimes stepping on a femur or a skull despite all efforts to avoid them sometimes slipping from crest to trough in the treacherous sand. They'd been at this for about an hour when a strange whirring and screeching caused them to spin about. The sky behind them had gone black with a mass of flying creatures. As the horde approached, Johnny realized it was made up of gigantic bats, perhaps two meters long in the body and with a wingspan of three to four meters. Their black wings and feet were tipped with nasty, obsidian-like talons. Covered with brown fur, the bats sported a sort of golden ruff around the neck, and their ears were tufted with the same color. Red eyes scanned the ground hungrily, and stiletto-sharp teeth gnashed as vulpine heads twisted back and forth.

"Okay, not your normal bat. But I think we can outrun them." He started pulling off his t-shirt, but a gasp from Carol made him freeze. Cresting the dunes in front of them were hundreds of snarling jaguars and pumas. A jamboree of that size was pretty much impossible in the real world, Johnny knew. It was probably held together by the enormous black puma that stood alone at the top of the nearest dune. Its size rivaled that of Xolotl, perhaps even dwarfing the hellhound. It tilted its sleek, massive head back and roared. The sound was unbearably beautiful to Johnny. His *tonal* surged within him.

"Crap. Okay." Johnny reacted quickly, by instinct. "Here's what we do. I'll shift and draw the cats away. You make a run for the next desert. When you're there, start calling me with *xoxal*. I'll circle back and find you."

"Wait!" Carol' cried. "I don't think it's a good idea for us to split up, Johnny. I'm pretty sure that's what he..."

Ignoring her, his *tonal* eager like never before, Johnny transformed and began to run, leaving his clothes, and Carol, forgotten. Twisting along the troughs between dunes, he gave full rein to his animal side, letting it push itself to extremes of speed and endurance. He reached deep within himself to the place that could hear Carol's voice and drew on the vast reserves of energy he found waiting for him. With impossible velocity, he made himself an irresistible target for the range of monstrous cats, and they poured through the wilderness after him, growling and hissing in rage.

Carol called to him faintly, twice, but their connection was soon severed by distance. The jamboree gradually spread itself across the dunes, the largest and fastest jaguars and pumas in front, their enormous paws eating up the yards between them and Johnny.

The alpha hurled roars and grunts and hisses at him that Johnny didn't understand. Slowly, as his *tonal* drew more and more *xoxal* to maintain its incredible speed and the noises coalesced into words.

"You cannot outrun me, young *nagual!*" the black puma was calling. "I am *Acolmiztli*, Lord of the *Balamija*, guardian of Mictlan. No living human has ever wormed his way past me!"

By impulse, Johnny shouted over his shoulder in the feline tongue, "Well, there's a first time for everything, little kitty!"

"*What* did you call me?" Acomiztli roared.

"Here, kitty-kitty! Come and get me!" With every fiber of his being, Johnny squeezed as much speed out of his jaguar form as magic permitted. Gouts of sand erupted all around him as he blazed through the low hills.

Then he emerged into a circular clearing, ringed by stunted trees and high dunes. In the middle, a dozen giants stood waiting. As he scrambled to slow down and avoid them, one shifted before his eyes, becoming a massive jaguar. Its right forepaw, the size of Johnny's entire body, slammed into him, hurling him against a dune.

Dazed, Johnny struggled to stand on legs that had suddenly gone slack. The other giants metamorphosed into equally large jaguars and surrounded him. Within seconds, Acomiztli leapt into the clearing, bellowing in anger. The black puma shook itself savagely and approached, its head low. The gigantic jaguars stepped aside.

Oh, no.

"So you are the mighty *nagual* come to wreak havoc upon us, are you? A puny, meager jaguar. More of an ocelot, if truth be told. It will give great pleasure to add you to the *Balamija*...as a groomer. You will spend the rest of your days picking ticks from the fur of your betters, human."

"Screw you," Johnny spat. He searched his memory of

animal documentaries for a term this feline would find horribly insulting. "I'll never bow down to your little glaring of gibs."

"Gibs, you call us? We shall see." Acomiztli turned to the shape-shifted giants. "Tukumbalam, Kotzbalam.Hold him down."

Fear crowded into his mind, sending both his human and animal souls into a tizzy. But his jerking attempts to escape were useless. Two of the huge jaguars used their oversized paws to hold him down. Their leader leaned close.

"Goodbye, *human*."

He placed his black forepaw on Johnny's neck and began to press. Slowly the wilderness began to fade to black. As if in a dream, he remembered Xolotl's words: "You may nonetheless be tempted to eat or sleep. Do *not*."

Great, Johnny thought. And then he slipped into unconsciousness.

T he young jaguar awakened, confused. Around him he sensed dozens of others, mostly males. It was strange for them to be all together. The young jaguar wanted to bolt.

"Ah, you're awake."

A medium-sized black cat—not a puma, but a melanistic jaguar—stood nearby.

"What...where...who?"

"They told me you might not remember anything. That's okay. I'm Itzocelotl. We just had a scrape with snatch-bats. You took a pretty serious blow to the head."

"Snatch-bats?"

"Yeah, the *kamasotzob*. Vicious, enormous? Our eternal rivals?"

The young jaguar shook his head. "Start smaller. Who are we? Who am I?"

"We're the *Balamija*, the feline guardians of the Underworld. We patrol this strip of wilderness, making sure nothing except dead human souls cross. And you? You're Chipohyoh, groomer for the *nahualocelomeh*."

Chipohyoh whisked his tail in confusion. Not even his own name stirred any recognition within him. "None of this seems familiar. Who are the *nahualocelomeh*?"

"There's one over there. See the really big jaguar ordering those pumas around? That's Tukumbalam. He is one of about twenty, all told. They're quite old, from the First Age. Were-jaguars, formed by mighty Tezcatlipoca to destroy the arrogant giants that the Feathered Snake had crafted to rule the earth. In fact, they're basically the first jaguars ever, based on the *tonal* of the Dark Lord himself."

Chipohyoh had to admit that the gigantic cat did look very powerful and very old. Its hide was crisscrossed with a netting of scars from millennia of battles. "Okay, so I'm their groomer. Like...removing nits and stuff?"

Itzocelotl pulled black lips back in a toothy smile. "Oh, yes."

"Doesn't sound like much fun."

"Oh, you love your job. You brag constantly about the time you get to spend with the Old Ones."

As Chipohyoh mulled this over, searching for any clue within himself that could contradict a reality that didn't *fit*, a huge black puma, only a bit smaller than the scarred *nahualocelotl*, padded in regally.

"A new cluster of souls is making its way along the Green

Road, victims of unexpected violence in southern Mexico, it seems. Tukumbalam, take your range and converge on them. Harry them until they are near breaking, then return."

"Of course, Lord. Always a pleasure to strip humanity from naïve, unprepared souls."

"And Tukumbalam? Take your groomer with you. Perhaps another blow to his head might set him to rights."

"As you wish. Chipohyoh, to me."

The young feline hurried to the were-jaguar's side.

"Itzocelotl, round up the rest. We leave upon my signal."

As the big cats dashed about, preparing for the sortie, Chipohyoh looked up at his enormous master and then at the retreating haunches of the black puma. "Sir, uh, who was that?"

The *nahualocelotl* looked down at him bemusedly. "That was Acomiztli, Lord of the Balamija. Now, quickly, I've a tick burrowing into my chest. Dig it out for me, will you?"

Feeling strangely humiliated, the young jaguar nuzzled the broad stretch of white between Tukumbalam's forelegs. He found the tick easily, seized it between his teeth and yanked it free.

"Perfect. Now let's away. Do try and keep up, little one."

They rounded a dune and found about a dozen jaguars and pumas of various sizes and colors awaiting orders. Tukumbalam roared his signal, and the felines exploded into movement. Chipohyoh ran alongside his master, the brutal pace surprisingly easy to maintain. *If I'm this fast, why am I just a groomer? It doesn't make any sense.*

Their journey seemed interminable, up and over and around dunes, over shattered bones, toward the Green Road (whatever that was). But running with his range gave Chipohyoh an unusual feeling of strength and surety: he was part of something bigger than him, with mighty brothers who would fight at his side. Though he could remember little else, the young jaguar felt that he had been alone for a long time, without a group to belong to. Despite his deep confusion, he was glad, at this moment, to be part of the *Balamija*.

Soon the dunes flattened into a plain of scalloped sand through which threaded a host of glowing lights, stretched single-file along the horizon. *Souls*, the young jaguar realized. *Human souls*. He felt an inexplicable pang of regret.

"Brothers!" cried Tukumbalam. "Let's make them drop their bones!"

The group descended on the souls, snarling and snapping. Chipohyoh saw as he approached the features etched faintly in the glow: men and women and children, fearful and confused. As the aggression of the felines increased, many of them shuddered, and bones fell tumbling.

Stripping their humanity away. They were trying to cling to the memory of who they were, I bet. And these...beasts...

Something inside him twisted. His sense of belonging evaporated like a mirage.

This is wrong. I'm wrong.

The young jaguar stood unmoving, staring at the harried travelers, glowing golden under the gloaming sky. From the souls, a shivering moaning filled the air.

"Come on, Chipohyoh. Do you want to be a groomer forever?" It was Itzocelotl, his teeth bared in a knowing grin. "You need to cut your teeth on one of these glow-worms."

Before he could respond, the young jaguar's innards

resounded with a bright, desperate call: *JOHNNY!*

"What the...Did you hear that?"

It's me, Johnny! Look up!

Unsure of what was going on, Chipohyoh raised his spotted head and saw a hundred or more dark forms streaking toward him through the sky.

"Snatch-bats!" growled a red puma, and hearing him, the group wheeled about to face their rivals. One of the enormous flying creatures spun away from the horde and descended toward Chipohyoh.

Come on! It's me! The big bat flying right at you is me, moron! Get moving!

How are you doing this? How can you speak into my mind like this?

Johnny, hello...it's the xoxal *magic! We spent hours earlier today, yesterday, whenever it was, communicating with our souls.*

What? Who are you? Why do you keep calling me 'Johnny'?

The bat landed in front of him and leaned its fox-like snout close to his. *I'm your sister Carol, for God's sake! You're Johnny, my brother!*

No. They told me my name is Chipohyoh. And how can I be the brother of a bat?

I'm not a bat. You're not a jaguar. We are humans, remember? What did they do to you?

All around them the *kamasotzob* were attacking the *Balamija*, obsidian claws sinking into feline flesh. The powerful jaws of the jaguars and pumas managed to crush some of the snatch-bats, but there were too many, and slowly the cats were routed or destroyed. The red puma, seeing Chipohyoh face to face with the enemy, came charging with jaws gaping at the creature that called itself Carol.

Here goes nothing, the voice whispered in the jaguar's head. The bat wrapped its wings about itself and pulled into a crouch. It closed its eyes and began to tremble and began to change. Its brown fur drew back into its skin, its wings shrunk to two arms, its golden ruff became frizzy brown hair and its snout squeezed down into the features of a human; a young girl.

"Johnny," she whimpered. "Save me."

Like an explosion, Johnny's human soul pulled away from its *tonal,* his memories restored. He leapt into the air, claws extended, and slammed into the puma before it clamped its jaws around his sister's head. They rolled in the sand, reaching for each other's throats, ears pressed back against their heads, snarls rasping their throats. The red puma, older and stronger, flipped Johnny onto his back. Just as its maw descended toward Johnny's jugular, a snatch-bat swooped down and sliced off its head. Johnny shoved the body away and stood.

Now come on! Carol projected at him. *This diversion's only going to last a little longer, Johnny!*

He followed the bat as it winged its way through the sky, turning toward the center of Mictlan and gradually curving back toward the Black Road.

I fell asleep, Johnny tried to explain. *Well, they knocked me out. When I woke up, I don't know...I couldn't remember who I was. They made me think I was one of them, Carol. I'm sorry.*

It's okay. I found you. We're safe. That's all that matters.

He stared up at her gruesome form. *But, how? I mean, I get that it's* xoxal *or whatever, but how'd you figure it out?*

Well, when you rushed off like a big dummy, I tried to bundle up your clothes and mine so I could carry them off. That took too long, and I found myself surrounded by the bats. I took a look at their talons and realized there was one on my necklace. Figuring it would make a good weapon, I grabbed it in my teeth and shifted. And guess what? I shifted into one of them.

Dude. I bet that surprised the crap out of them.

Uh, yeah. After a few minutes, I realized I could communicate with them. It took me a while, but I convinced them that if they really wanted to hurt the...uh...

Balamija?

...yeah, them, that they should wait until they weren't all together. After I hid our clothes, I helped them track you guys, in wolf form. I figured that eventually you'd be left alone or the Balamija would split up somehow. When you ran off with them toward the Green Road, I saw my opportunity. I got the bats to wait until you guys were so far away from the rest that they couldn't come running, and then I suggested that we attack. You know the rest.

They were approaching dunes that reached higher and higher, merging into rocky hills and steppes.

I hid our clothes up there, near the edge of the next desert.

The bats let you come here before tracking us?

Well, with an escort. They didn't totally trust me, but they hate the jaguars and pumas more.

Okay, so this isn't easy, Johnny said, slipping on some scree. *Would it be better if I flew?*

Carol circled back and landed beside him. Examining his bracelet, she nodded.

There's a screech owl feather right there. Put it in your mouth and let the tonal find its new form. Just step away, is all. Nothing to it.

Lifting his foreleg, Johnny used his raspy tongue to pull the feather into his mouth. He felt the eager joy of his tonal and stayed out of its way as it shifted fur into feathers, lightened bones, deleting mass by some unknown magic means. His talons gripped the rock and he spread enormous wings. His transformed eyes, even keener than the jaguar's, made every detail of the shadowy landscape pop into sharp relief.

Wow. I'm a freaking lechuza!

And with two powerful flaps, he was flying.

CHAPTER ELEVEN

C arol led her feathered brother up the cliffs to the cave where she had stowed their clothing. They took the bundles in their claws and continued their upward spiraling. The sheer rock face seemed to go on forever, and the updrafts that bore them aloft grew thinner and less reliable until they found themselves having to draw on *xoxal* to give them strength enough to beat their wings and ascend into the colder and higher layers of atmosphere.

Finally they made it to the top. Perching, exhausted, on boulders that lined the edge of the cliff, they looked out over a vast and snowy mesa. An icy wind swept toward them, ruffling their feathers, chilling their blood. Distant swirls suggested storms of great violence.

Okay, I think my wolf form can handle this cold better. Turn around, though. I have to get my bundle tied around me. You'd better do the same.

What? Stand naked in this cold? Are you crazy?

Well, you can shift right into the jaguar, but you'll have to carry it in your mouth. Not fun.

I've got a better idea. Hang on.

Carol watched as her brother's owl form shuddered and morphed into something halfway between boy and jaguar: covered with fur, but humanoid.

"Stop *tonal* halfway," he growled in a bestial voice. "Warmer."

Clever. As her brother tied his clothes bundle about his waist and finished shifting, Carol tried the same trick. Her *tonal* quivered in frustration, but by concentrating hard, she was able to be a wolf-girl long enough to square her clothes away as well. Then she slipped completely into her lupine shape, complete with an extra winter undercoat. The cold still nipped at her, but it was bearable.

They began to trudge across the snow, circling around drifts that had built up near boulders or dead trees. As they advanced, the wind's velocity seemed to increase steadily until they were forcing their way almost blindly through flurries, guided only by their innate sense of direction. Soon the constant moaning of the wind gave way to something fiercer, a monstrous howling that made the plateau itself shudder beneath their paws.

What the...Do you feel that, Carol?

Yes. And, whatever it is, it's definitely getting closer.

Squinting through the snowflakes, Carol suddenly saw it: an enormous white whirlwind, twisting its way along the wintery mesa, ripping apart boulders and trees. It was headed straight for them.

I think we need to run.

Johnny looked into the distance and saw the snowy tornado as well. *Uh, I agree.*

They slanted sideways, running counterclockwise (based on Xolotl's brief comments, Carol imagined each desert as a circle, like the ones her Pre-AP English teacher said existed in Hell). The whirlwind, seeming to sense them, changed direction abruptly and began to follow.

It's coming after us, Johnny!

Freaking great. Look: there's a huge outcropping of rock to our right. Seems there's a hollow spot in the center, kind of like a cave. We can ride out the storm in there.

Carol wasted no time replying. She pushed her wolf form to its limits, leaping into the space among the rocks just ahead of her brother. They huddled together in the dark, panting, the warmth of their close proximity a welcome change from the bitter cold. The grinding approach of the whirlwind grew louder and louder.

Thank God we can communicate soul to soul, Carol projected. We wouldn't be able to hear each other with this noise.

Yeah. And we're lucky to find shelter. That tornado means busin—

The twisting whiteness struck the surrounding rocks and lifted them effortlessly away. The twins stared up into its funnel, a blank black space around which swirled snow, sand and shredded trees.

Carol moved without further hesitation, rushing away as fast as her four legs would carry her, Johnny right on her heels. With what seemed like a howl of frustration, the whirlwind changed directions and followed them again.

Dude, it's like the thing is alive!

Or being controlled by someone, Carol suggested. She was certain now that whatever had their mother was actively trying to keep them from reaching the center of Mictlan. As if to confirm her suspicions, two more freezing cyclones appeared on the horizon, moving quickly. The three would converge on her and Johnny within minutes.

Glancing down at the necklace that dangled about her neck, Carol took stock of her possible forms. None were faster than the wolf. She thought about becoming a snatch-bat again, trying to fly above the twisters, but it seemed a foolish plan, unlikely to end well. A glance at the bracelet round Johnny's upper foreleg revealed a similar dilemma.

We need help, or we're going to die. Quetzalcoatl, do you hear me? Tonantzin? God? Mother Mary? Please come to our aid. We want to complete this mission, truly, want to save our mother, stop the dark forces. But if we die now, we're pretty much useless. We can't do this alone. Please.

Thundering from between the two new tornadoes came Xolotl, insanely fast, the wrinkled skin of his face blown back in a grimace that was both fearful and funny. Skidding to a stop in front of them, he shouted against the wailing winds: "Shift into something with opposable thumbs and get on my back quickly!"

Carol saw only one possibility. She took a little desiccated black digit in her mouth. In moments she was a rather large raccoon, clambering up the side of the gigantic red hellhound. A similarly oversized spider monkey swung onto Xolotl's back behind her.

Aw, Johnny's found his true inner form, she joked.

Ya cállate, méndigo mapache. Now I know who steals my sweets from my room when I'm asleep. Bandit. You don't even have thumbs, just really flexible paws. You might have to use your little teeth, Rocky Raccoon.

"Hang on!" Xolotl called. Their hands gripped folds of his skin, and he exploded into movement just as the three cyclones came together. The hellhound moved with supernatural speed, sending up walls of snow and sand in the wake of his passing. Carol clung for dear life. When Xolotl began to ascend into the bleak mountains from which the biting wind blew, she nearly slipped, but her brother's prehensile tail snagged her and pulled her close.

Careful, sis. I've got you. Four opposable thumbs and a grabby tail: I can hold on for the both of us.

Eventually they'd climbed high enough into the mountains that the cyclones could only beat uselessly against the slopes. Xolotl ducked into a large cavern, and Carol scurried off into a dark recess to change. It felt good to be a human girl again, to feel denim and cotton against her skin, to stand erect and have a voice.

Of course, it's crazy cold in here, but I need to talk to him. We deserve answers.

Johnny had already changed and was huddling close to a fire that danced on the surface of a ring of rocks, presumably via magic worked by Xolotl. She hurried to the warmth, rubbing her hands with momentary delight before turning to the hellhound.

"Thanks for saving us."

"You're welcome. I was already on my way, but I heard your prayer and came as fast as possible."

Johnny opened his mouth, his eyebrow raised as if to make a sarcastic comment, but Carol waved him to silence. "Xolotl, the first two deserts almost got us."

"I know, Carolina. Our eyes are on you. We—"

"Your eyes..." She swallowed the anger she felt burning in the pit of her stomach. "But you guys didn't intervene. I could have been lost in that dark forever. Johnny could have forgotten who he was forever. I need to understand why you would risk us like that if we're so important."

Sighing, Xolotl shifted into his human form. He mumbled a few words and the fur he clenched about him swirled into normal if old-fashioned clothes: boots, jeans, a woolen shirt and duster. At a gesture, a slouch hat appeared in his hands, and he set it on his dirty blond hair.

"It's easier to chat like this," he said, sitting on a nearby pile of rocks.

"Dude, you look like a cowboy." Johnny had a real dislike for Western clothing, partly because everyone in their dad's family was so Tex-Mex or country and was always pressuring him to jump on that bandwagon.

"Yes, well, this was how I dressed the last time I incarnated. It's easier to conjure up." He nodded in Carol's direction. "Okay. Let's talk about what you've faced thus far. Carolina, the black silence that attempted to possess you is *cehualli*, the dark shadow magic of Tezcatlipoca. It is his entropic response to *teotl*, the creative power that binds the universe together. You fought it off, amazingly, by using a *teocuicatl*, a sacred hymn that repels chaos, destruction and entropy. What I don't understand is where that song came from."

Carol cleared her throat to hide her emotion. "My dad. I was attacked this way five years ago, and my dad sang a song to help me get past my fear. He only sang one verse, over and over, but the entire song came to me there in the darkness."

The man scratched at the stubble on his chin. "I suppose I just don't remember, but someone in your father's family must have been a *cuicuani*, a sacred singer. They passed the gift on to him, and it is now accessible to you. That's good news. Songs are powerful defenses."

"Yay," said Johnny weakly, holding one of his bare feet toward the fire. "Carol's a Jedi diva."

"Hush, dork."

"Strong in this one is the *teotl*," Johnny croaking, aping Yoda's voice. "Yodel she will against the Aztec Sith and their *cehualli* light sabers."

Carol punched her brother in the shoulder. "I'm trying to be serious, Johnny. And he doesn't even get your cutesy pop culture references."

"That I don't," Xolotl confirmed. "But I do understand what happened to Juan Ángel among the Balamija. First, his *tonal* responded to the call of Acomiztli, one of the most powerful beings in Mictlan. That's what made him foolishly to attempt to draw the creatures away. That and a newly blossoming desire to *belong*. For most of your childhood you have been inseparable. Your mother's disappearance has pulled you so far apart that you, Juan Ángel, have been excluding yourself from groups of boys your age, while Carol had managed to build a support system of friends that helped her deal with the loss, not only of your mother, but of you, her best friend. The *Balamija* took advantage of your longing to once again be a member of a group."

Carol noticed Johnny's eyes, downcast and embarrassed at this revelation. She suddenly felt ashamed herself. *He needed me, and I pushed him away. My best friend.*

Xolotl pushed his hat a little farther back on his head. "Then, Juan Ángel, you did precisely what I had warned you both *not* to do: you fell asleep."

"Wait, *they knocked me out*, cowboy. Not the same thing."

"Yes, but you put yourself in that position. When either of you becomes unconscious in this place, your human and animal souls will combine and you lose your memories."

Johnny gritted his teeth. "Great. So Carol's awesome because she sang away the darkness, but I suck because I let myself get merged or whatever."

"Don't get defensive. You should have been stuck that way forever, Juan Ángel, a random jaguar in the *Balamija* for eternity, or until one of the snatch-bats killed you. But you managed to peel your human self away from your *tonal*. How?"

Carol looked intently at Johnny as he remembered. "It was Carol. She…she was in danger. I *had* to be me again. To save her."

"Good. Your love for your family is a powerful source of *teotl* as well, and that magic triggers the uncommon *xoxal* you both possess."

Giggling, Carol mouthed *love Jedi* at Johnny, and he cracked a smile. Returning her attention to Xolotl, she expressed what was on both their minds.

"Couldn't you have told us this stuff earlier? You're not a very good guide, you know."

"It's the way of Quetzalcoatl. If you are given too much help, you aren't acting of your own free will. There's much he could do to interfere in human affairs. But he refuses to. People have to be free to discover the truth, to make mistakes. To believe lies, if you choose to. Like this place. For centuries, Tezcatlipoca spread a vicious lie among the Mexica and other Aztec tribes that souls are destroyed at the center of Mictlan. As I've told you, in reality they pass Beyond, where neither Quetzalcoatl nor Tezcatlipoca have any sway. But the Dark Lord thrives on despair and chaos. He made your ancestors believe that everything enduring about their personalities would fade away at the end of their four-year journey. For this reason there was no ancestor worship among the

Mexica. Four years after their deaths, people's names were forgotten. Grave sites were unmarked. A deep, existential sadness pervaded the lives of those who believed this lie."

This was one of the most depressing things Carol had ever heard. It echoed some of her father's own concerns about the Aztec empire; his articles criticizing this and other elements of their worldview had caused quite a furor among certain academic circles.

"But we stayed distant, even then. Because humans must find hope on their own. You must face the darkness alone. You've been given the tools, but the fight is yours." He stood, pressing his hat more tightly upon his head, adjusting the string beneath his chin. "And that's why I have to leave you now. I will not say the coming challenges are easier than the first three. That would be a lie. I will promise you, however, that if you stay together and put your love for family above all else, you will make it through to the heart of Mictlan. There the greatest barrier to your happiness awaits you. I believe in you both, little brother and sister. I know that you are strong enough to stand when everyone else would cringe and bow.

"Fight for your mother's freedom, twins. I'll see you on the other side."

And he stepped into the darkness outside the cave and disappeared.

CHAPTER TWELVE

Johnny stared for a long time at the entrance to the cave, Xolotl's words echoing in his head. The weight of the work before them suddenly settled on his shoulders. Physically and emotionally, he was exhausted. He wanted nothing more than to sit down beside the fire and rest for days.

So instead he shrugged and beckoned to Carol. "Time to get moving. Six more of these stupid deserts left."

Carol sighed. "I feel like I'm at the Mall, going and in and out of changing rooms."

"About that. I just wanted to half-shift into the jaguar-boy or whatever. I think I can hold that form long enough to get down the mountainside. Haunted ruins, that's what's next. Do we really need an animal form for ghosts?"

"Okay, it's worth a try."

Johnny let his *tonal* come forward, stopping it partway through the transformation. With most of his attention on maintaining that unnatural blend of human and beast, he exited the cave and made his way along the dark path that threaded through the peaks and down the other side of the freezing mountains. The wolf-girl followed close behind him, her labored breathing a sign of how difficult she found her transitional shape. Before too long, however, the howling, icy winds were gone, and the twins reverted to human form with a sigh of relief.

The mountain slope was gradual and carpeted with dead grass. Johnny's feet were pricked from time to time by burrs and thorns, but beyond that, the descent was pretty easy.

Carol finally broke their sustained silence by clearing her throat.

"Johnny, I, uh, want to apologize. I haven't been there for you like I need to be. I took refuge in my friends and left you pretty much alone. That was wrong."

Johnny waved her concerns away. "Oh, that wasn't your fault, Carol. I'm the one who didn't want to share his feelings, remember? I just thought that if I didn't talk about it, that if I kept my pain really close, then Mom would be alive in me, you know? I was, this is kind of stupid, but I was afraid that if I talked about it, I'd start accepting it, and then I would move on. I didn't want to, you know?"

"Yes, I get you. Well, the good thing is, we're a team again, right? Just like when we stood up to those bullies that one time. What were we, five years old?"

Johnny thought of the two of them, facing down a gang of kids three years older than them. He laughed at the image. "Yeah. Stupid Martínez kids. Their parents had them so spoiled, huh? But we didn't give them our toys that day, and we ran them off. That was pretty cool. Sure, Carol. We're a team again. The Garza Twins. All we need are rings and a monkey."

"What?"

Johnny pretended to be shocked. "Dude, I keep telling you... you need to watch more classic cartoons. Filling your head with a bunch of boring history is going to drive you nuts."

"No, listening to your weird pop-culture allusions is what is going to drive me nuts."

"Dude, you're a girl! What do you even talk about with Nikki and all them? Because, yeah, your friends don't seem all up on all this stuff you know, like, pre-Colombian political systems and stuff. Just saying."

"Well, we don't sit around talking about action films and 70s cartoons. We, you know, talk about..."

Johnny snapped his fingers. "Boys. You talk about boys. Predictable."

Carol flushed red, and Johnny laughed. *Oh, man. When she starts dating, we're going to have so much fun, Dad and me. Threatening the stupid punks and all.*

"Uh, if you're done mocking me, you might look down there." Carol gestured at the valley that now spread below them. Its dark red sands were dotted with ruined stone structures of all sizes, from small homes to enormous cathedrals.

"Okay. Ruins. And ghosts. What can we expect?"

"Based on what they've already tried, they'll want to freak us out and/or separate us. So, uh, don't let the ghosts freak you out, and stick close to me."

Johnny smirked. "Yeah, why don't *you* stick close to *me*, huh?"

"We'll stick close to each other, alright?" Her eyes flashed lupine yellow.

"Don't get all *esponjada*, Carol. I'm just kidding."

They soon found themselves ambling along among the ruins. The buildings seemed impossibly old, inscriptions and decorations worn nearly invisible by the passage of time. Johnny studied their unusual architecture, not detecting any signs of the major trends in either European or Mesoamerican design. Granted, he was still an amateur, but as far as he could tell, the structures had not been made by human hands. The dimensions were off, the symmetry awry, the engineering techniques were frankly, alien.

"Carol, you're the Mexican history buff...How many ages have gone by, in Aztec mythology?"

"We're in the...fifth, I think. Yes. This is the fifth sun. The last age."

"What happened to end the other ones?"

"Oh, uh, destruction? Remember what Xolotl told us. Some gods, mainly Quetzalcoatl, kept trying to create intelligent beings, but then they'd get wiped out."

Johnny nodded, running his fingers along the frame of an enormous doorway. "The *Balamija* have these huge were-jaguars that killed off the giants of the First Age. That's what one cat told me. I wonder...maybe these are buildings from all the way back then."

Carol shrugged. "Who knows? Or maybe from one of the other ages."

Unbidden, a thought rose to Johnny's consciousness. "Oh, man."

"What?"

"Xolotl. He said it was mainly Tezcatlipoca doing the destroying, right?"

Carol swallowed hard. "Yeah."

"And what about our world? The fifth one. What do the legends say?"

Carol squinted, as if thinking hard. "I'm not sure, Johnny. I'm more interested in *actual history*, not *mythology*, you know."

Raising an eyebrow, Johnny gestured around them. "Dude, it seems to me that mythology and history? Same thing."

"Okay. Touché or whatever. Your point?"

"My point is: what if that's what he wants to destroy the world? Maybe he needs to kill us or something to make it happen."

Carol's face went pallid. "Or maybe he needs our help. Our *xoxal*."

"Why the heck would we help him? That's crazy."

"Maybe that's why he's got Mom, Johnny. So he can blackmail us."

The idea was sobering. Johnny tried to imagine himself choosing between his mother's life and the destruction of the entire world. *Screw that. We'll find another way. We'll beat Mr. Chaos-and-Dark-Magic. Even if he is a god.*

"And you'll fail her," a voice muttered nearby. Johnny whipped his head around and saw his grandmother, fluttering spectrally in the doorway of a nearby building.

"*Abuela* Helga?" Carol whispered.

"Yes, it's me, you cold-hearted child. You sent me to my death, so you shouldn't be surprised to find me here, in the Land of Shades."

"Wait," Johnny said. "*We* sent you to your death? But you just *let go*, didn't you? You had been holding on, waiting to tell us what we were. Then you escaped…"

"Oh, you're right that I was holding on," the phantasm hissed, writhing angrily. "For years I waited for you to visit me, trapped in that broken body. But you were too good to come across the border, weren't you? Too young and full of life to spend time with an old, crippled woman."

Tears slipped down Carol's face. "Oh, *abuelita*, I'm so sorry! I was selfish and unthinking..."

"Yes!" raged the apparition. "You were cruel! And as a result, you didn't learn of your abilities. Your mother had no one who could help her fight off the dark that crept round your home and dragged her down. This is *all your fault!*"

Carol was openly weeping now, and Johnny's chest felt like it would burst. *This isn't right, though. She wouldn't treat us like this. She wouldn't even feel that way. Not abue.*

"Shhh, Carol," he muttered. "Stop crying. It's not her." Turning to the specter, he repeated with more confidence. "You're not her. You're some demon pretending to be her. Well, you can go tell your master I said his little tricks are worth crap. We're coming for our mother, and we're coming for *him*. He wants *xoxal*, we're going to give it to him. But he ain't going to like it. You tell him that, you fake. Tell him to stick his *cehualli* where the sun don't shine."

"Fool. Don't listen to me then. Ignore me like you've done for years. You'll pay the price, and so will my daughter."

With that, the ghostly form faded away. Johnny put his arm around his sister, urging her to continue walking.

"I know it wasn't her," Carol managed to say at last. "But what she was saying was true."

"Maybe. But our real grandmother forgave us. You saw that. You felt it when we ran with her freed *tonal* under the moonlight. Whatever that thing was, it just used our own guilt against us.

And when other quote-unquote *ghosts* appear, they're going to do the same. So get yourself psyched up. I'm sure this is just the beginning of the attack."

They continued along the Black Road, which for a time became the cracked cobblestones of some broad ancient highway. Lined with massive headless statues and broad, shattered plinths, the road led them deeply into the remains of a mighty city, overgrown with thorny black vines. Pale moths and beetles scurried over fallen granite blocks, and the eyes of vultures and ravens followed the twins as they went by.

They were passing under a bridge-like structure that stretched over the highway when another specter stepped onto the cobblestones before them. Unmistakable in his black suit, tortoise shell glasses and meager goatee, the man stared at them sadly.

It was their father.

Putting out an arm to stop his sister, Johnny shook his head. "Forget it. We know you're not really him. Don't even bother. First place, he isn't even dead."

"Oh, Johnny," the phantom whispered, his hazel eyes watery. "Of course I wasn't dead the last time you saw me. But I couldn't bear to be without your mother anymore. Once I knew you two were safe with her sister, there was nothing keeping me from putting an end to my pain."

Carol clenched her fists. "You shut up. Our father would *never* kill himself."

"Wouldn't I? All those times you checked in on me, found me drunk and weeping in my study...Did you really never think that I might consider this option? I'm sorry, Sweetie. I know I always told you to stand strong against the darkness. But at heart, I guess I'm a coward. The worst thing is that I know the truth now. Your mother is here, trapped. If only you had been faster. I suppose some of my weakness is in you, too. But now it's too late. Say you rescue her. What will you three return to?" The apparition began to weep. "Forgive me, kids!"

Johnny was filled with rage. He knew this thing to be a mirage drawn from their own fears, but it felt so real having reached into their hearts in the most cunning of ways. Ironically it triggered the opposite reaction of what Tezcatlipoca and his servants had intended.

"You are *not* my dad. My dad loves me, and he's struggling right now to get his head sorted so that he can give Carol and me a normal life. You can point out my weaknesses and screw-ups all you want, demon, but you are *not* Dr. Oscar Garza. You don't even come freaking close. You couldn't even tie the man's dress shoes, you piece of scum."

With an expression of sadness on his face and a disappointed shake of his head, the specter oozed into a towering pillar and could be seen no more. Carol, who looked really spooked by the somber pronouncements of the fakes, allowed Johnny to lead her along. The road led into a huge plaza ringed by thick tree stumps that had petrified over millennia. A strange, echoing animal sound flittered through the air, and Johnny felt Carol stiffen beside him. Then he heard her gasp.

"Oh, my God, Johnny. It's Puchi."

Johnny turned to where she indicated and saw the ghostly image of their favorite dog. Puchi had been at their side since they'd arrived from the hospital as newborns until she had died of old age two years ago. It had been devastating to watch her go blind and slow down till one day they'd discovered her, curled up under a grapefruit tree, her body cold and lifeless. *And when Dad buried her out back, we cried like we had lost our best friend. Come to think of it, that's pretty much what had happened.*

The apparition was young and healthy, though, and ran about them with unbridled joy. Carol knelt and called to her with a soft whistle. Puchi rushed at them then bounded away playfully the way she once had when she wanted to be chased.

"Carol," Johnny warned as his sister stood, "don't even think about it. This is a trap."

His sister's voice was calm but distant. "I'm not stupid, Johnny. Of course it's a trap. But it's coming no matter what, so why don't we just play along? That way we have a few minutes with her, even if she isn't real."

With a shrug and a sigh, Johnny went along with her. They followed the dog off the Black Road, onto an intersecting boulevard lined with thorny black rose bushes that led toward a white tower looming in the near distance. As they came closer, Johnny saw that the building was a single piece, as if cement had been poured into an impossibly massive mold. There were no apparent doors or windows, only a jagged parapet ringing the very top. The spectral canine dove into a tangle of silvery, wilted herbs that encircled the tower's base, and the twins came to a stop.

Johnny shuddered with realization. "Carol, that tower was carved from bone. From a single, freaking *huge* bone."

"What sort of creature has a bone that size, Johnny? That's got to be thirty meters tall."

"Well, I'm guessing whatever it was doesn't exist anymore."

They walked around the base of the tower, looking for the ghost dog. There were no markings of any kind anywhere on the surface of the stele and no sign of Puchi's doppelganger.

"Weird. They used her to lure us here," Johnny mused aloud, "so where's the trap?"

"There's no trap, kids."

Despite six months without hearing it, Johnny recognized the clipped, lightly accented voice immediately. Verónica Quintero de Garza stepped from within the ivory white tower, a haunting smile on her cracked lips. Her dark hair was standing out wildly in all directions, her brown eyes sunken deeply into a face stripped bare of its normal elegant make-up.

"I sent the vision of Puchi to draw you here," she continued, her hands reaching out to them. Johnny noted that her slacks and blouse were badly stained and torn. "I don't have much time. They use this tower to send demons against you, trying to make you despair. In moments they'll return to try again. So let me be quick, *mis amores.*

"*Han sido muy valientes, los dos.* Very brave. I'm prouder than you can imagine. But you cannot continue. The danger is too great. Even if you get past all obstacles, when you stand before him, you'll be weakened beyond belief. And he will twist you, make you give your power to him. Rather than risk that, I'm willing to sacrifice myself."

Carol, who had been trembling for a while, suddenly cried out. "No, Mom! You can't!"

Johnny shook his head. *It's a trick. Has to be.*

"This is nuts. They're really desperate, Carol. To give themselves away like this? We scare them."

"What are you talking about? Johnny, that's not a fake! That's *Mom!*"

The phantom turned loving eyes on him. "Yes, Johnny, listen to your sister. It's really me."

Johnny laughed, finally certain. "Oh, they're scared, alright. And scared people always screw up. It's not her, Carol, and now you know it."

Carol closed her eyes and nodded. "I guess...I guess I just wanted to believe..."

Their mother's double narrowed her eyes. "Kids? What are you going on about? You need to leave, now. Travel counterclockwise until you come to the Green Road, and then follow it back. You'll emerge..."

"Carol, sing."

She stared at him, her mouth open. "Sing *what?*"

"Anything. One of Mom's lullabies. *Use the Force, Luke.*"

Closing his eyes, Johnny began to picture his mother, dressed to the nines, her hair perfectly done, make-up flawless, all 168 centimeters of her joyously alive as she walked along an exhibit of her sculptures. In his mind, she turned to him and beckoned.

Carol's voice began to echo in that damned wasteland, at first tentative, then with greater confidence and beauty, sounding out clear, powerful notes that seemed to set the tower thrumming:

> *A la ru ru niño*
> *A la ru ru ya.*
> *Tus sueños te protegen*
> *De la oscuridad.*

A la ru ru niño
A la ru ru ya,
Porque viene el coco
Y te comerá.

Y si no te come,
Él te llevará;
Y si no te lleva,
Quién sabe qué hará.

Este lindo niño
Ya se va a dormir
Háganle la cuna
De rosa y jazmín.

Toronjil de plata,
Torre de marfil,
Arrullen al niño
Que ya quiere dormir.

As the dark lullaby flooded his soul with memories, his mother's face loomed larger and larger, filling his mental vision. Her eyes crinkled beautifully, and she called to him, as she always did.

"*Juan Ángel, ven acá, amor.*"

Not *Johnny*. Never Johnny. And in that moment, the love he had been bottling up within him—fearful of forgetting, frightened of losing the sound of her voice forever—came rushing out like a tide, and he instinctively directed it at the specter before him, shouting with authority he had never imagined he could muster:

"Show us what you really are!"

A muffled shriek made him open his eyes. Before them their mother's form *peeled away*, revealing a pterodactyl-like monster with the backward-bent legs of a rooster. Its human-like face was shattered and scarred, and as it spread its leathery wings, it shrieked again in bitter rage.

"Behold Ixpuztec, master of faces!" Its voice was like the snapping of dry bones. "And now I shall gladly rip yours from your foolish heads you sniveling brats!"

Ixpuztec's wings beat the air twice, lifting about four meters. Then the demon dove at them, razor-sharp talons first.

Seizing the screech owl feather, Johnny transformed, clutching at his clothes and spiraling away on an updraft. Carol was now a snatch-bat, and Johnny caught a glimpse of her as she raked her own obsidian claws against Ixpuztec's already ruined face.

Fly, Johnny, fly! I'm right behind you!

Catching a strange, rushing current, Johnny corrected his trajectory and then hurtled parallel to the Black Road. Ahead the sky wavered and seethed, like summer air above the blacktop. Twisting his agile owl head, he saw his sister gliding behind him. Below her, rushing upward, was a cloud of black: Ixpuztec, accompanied by thousands upon thousands of ravens and vultures.

Well, Carol, we're almost past this desert. I see the next one up ahead. Lava plains, right? Scarface and his feathered friends can't cross over. We're almost in the clear.

The warm current soon drew them to a chain of volcanoes that appeared to serve as a border between the two circles of Mictlan. The mass of demonic birds had almost caught up when the twins winged their way between two bubbling calderas. An explosion of super-heated gas and ash fried the hundreds of ravens and vultures who had not turned aside at the last minute.

Wow, that was close, Carol projected.

Yeah. Those birds got fried extra crispy. We just need a jalapeño and some charro beans, and we'd have an awesome feast.

Gross!

Yeah, well, after who-knows-how-many hours or days in the Underworld, I'm really working up a craving for some comfort food, you know. Anyway, four down, five to go. I think we're really getting a hang of this, yeah? And look, just a bunch of lava flows. Great updrafts. I think we'll get through this desert quick.

He glanced down just in time to see the enormous flying wyrm before it wrapped itself around him and plunged toward the fiery plains.

CHAPTER THIRTEEN

Carol screamed in her ragged bat voice as the winged serpent lunged through the air, seizing her brother in coils of shimmering red and gold. Pulling her own wings tight against her body, she dropped like a stone after them. The wind whistled past her sensitive ears in a warbling wail, but before she could reach Johnny, another huge iridescent snake emerged from the sulfuric mists and plucked her from the air with the tip of its twisting tail.

Terrified, she squirmed around inside the serpent's unalterable grip, almost shifting before she remembered the bat was her only flight-capable option if she got free. She soon realized she couldn't reach her animal talismans anyway, so she worked to calm herself down. It was difficult. She knew she was panicking, but couldn't help remembering what had gotten her here. Overcoming the *cehualli* attack, convincing the *kamasotzob* to help her, being saved by Xolotl from the icy whirlwinds only to watch him abandon her...All of those trials paled beside the psychological ordeal of facing the doppelgangers of her loved ones and hearing their dreadful but inescapably true pronouncements.

Dad said that souls had their humanity stripped away, bit by bit, till only a wisp was left. I can't let that happen to me. I've got to hold on to who I am.

Her captor veered left and then right, avoiding the super-heated blasts of steam from below. Carol, her mind calmer, waited to discover where the creature was taking her. *Hopefully Johnny will be there, too, and together we can figure out a way to escape.*

The wyrm's wings beat the hot air for several minutes before it began to descend into the large, bowl-like caldera of a smoking volcano. Craning her head back, Carol saw that the crater contained a steaming lake, at the center of which stood an island of volcanic rock. Lava dribbled from a sort of shattered hill, draining down into the water in a glowing ribbon. Along the fiery stream a massive black temple had been erected, its ziggurat steps reflecting the red with hellish fierceness. It was atop this temple that the flying serpent released Carol and landed, coiling its body beneath itself and digging winged claws into the black stone to support its upper half. It had no legs.

Tightening her own talons around her clothes, Carol spread her wings, ready to attempt her escape.

"That would be quite useless." The voice was smooth and aristocratic, employing the cultured tones of a Spanish prince or Aztec emperor. Carol lowered her wings a bit as a man ascended the steps to stand a few yards away from her. He was tall and thin and extravagantly dressed. On his head sat a golden circlet, part of a headdress from which a ridge of white feathers emerged, followed by blue-green plumes that swept backwards down the black, downy cape draped over his broad shoulders. His skin was the faint blue of the dead except for strange golden tracings: ancient glyphs tattooed on cheeks, chest and forearms. Around his eyes was a black mask that glittered with pinpricks of blue fire like the glowing azure of his irises; a loincloth of the same material hung to his knees. In his right hand he clutched a sinister-looking dart and in his left, a broad shield at the center of which had been mounted an obsidian mirror. Carol saw her bat form reflected in its depths and quailed.

He smiled. "To be sure, I invite you to make the attempt. My fire serpent, Xiuhcoatl, would easily recapture you. However, even if he did not, I could bring you back down with little effort. In fact," he pronounced with a slight tipping of his shield, "you are now quite unable to escape."

Irritated by his mocking tone, Carol flapped leathery wings, only to discover that he had been telling the truth. Some sorcery kept her talons firmly attached to the top of the pyramid.

"We need to converse, you and I, Carolina. Return to your normal form. Now."

Carol stared at him with red eyes, and then gestured with her wing.

"Ah, you wish for me to turn around? Childish thing. Do you truly believe me interested in your unripe flesh? Very well. Dress quickly."

He gave her his back, and it was her *tonal* that rather randomly sensed his cape was covered in eaglet down. Shifting into her human form, she pulled on undergarments, pants and shirt. Xiuhcoatl hissed softly, smoke curling from its nostrils. Carol jerked her chin up at it in a defiant gesture, and it flicked its forked tongue at her hungrily. As she bent to slip on her socks, she noticed a single shimmering scale that had flaked free of the winged serpent, lying a meter away. The seed of a plan began to germinate.

She was slipping into her sneakers when the masked blue man faced her again.

"Better. Do you know who I am, Carolina Garza?"

"No. Batman? A *lucha libre* wrestler?"

His grim smile conveyed a desire to break her bones slowly. "I am *Huitzilopochtli*, you sniveling wench. Resurrected warrior of the south. Lord of sun and fire and battle. Do you know me?"

Carol recognized the name immediately. Her father had told her many stories of the arrival of the Aztecs in the Valley of Mexico. She had been fascinated by the nomadic Mexica tribe and how they had been forced to leave kingdom after kingdom until settling at Lake Texcoco, and how they had worked as mercenaries for decades until forming the Triple Alliance that in a century had conquered the entire Valley of Mexico. Dr. Garza had written several monographs about the first Moctezuma. That pre-Colombian king had sought to erase the history of the nations he conquered and replace it with a glorified tale of Aztec dominance. His brother the high priest had developed a religious doctrine that required greater and greater human sacrifice to stave off disaster. They had elevated their bloodthirsty god of war to the head of their pantheon.

"Sure, I know who you are. The god the Aztecs worshipped above all others. The one who led them out of Aztlán, down into Mexico."

Huitzilopochtli's smile broadened. "Very good! I see your father taught you well, Carolina."

She stopped in the middle of tying her left sneaker. "How do you know about my dad?"

"I am a *god*, little one. Of course I know."

Carol scoffed. "You're a *cruel* god. By the time they got to the Valley of Mexico, the Aztecs had really changed, huh? Human sacrifice...that was your idea, wasn't it? Conquering weaker nations, slaughtering men, women and children to make sure the sun would rise. All that tragedy."

The god made a dismissive gesture. "Oh, enough. You and your Western notions of right and wrong. My people were not some pasty European race. They were warriors. The conquest of Mexico was their birthright."

"Whatever." Carol shook her head and stood, her shoelaces tied. "What's right is right and what's wrong is wrong, no matter what. Cruelty and murder are evil *anywhere*. Some god you turned out to be. My dad says you were probably just a human leader who got elevated to divine status after his death."

Huitzilopochtli crossed the space between them in three broad strides. "Do I look like a mere man to you, child? For a thousand years I walked among the people that would become the Mexica, sustained by *cehualli*, preparing the way for their dark destiny. No human elevated me to divinity, you stinking wolf. I won apotheosis by my own hands. I was translated to a perfect state through the power I alone learned to wield."

Carol suddenly understood. "Human sacrifice. That's how you got access to the shadow magic. And that's why you needed the empire, the Flower Wars, the temple steps all covered in blood and your name at the top of the list of gods...Tell me the truth. You didn't come up with the idea by yourself, did you? Somebody else showed you how to use *cehualli* and how to prep the Mexica, right? Maybe Tezcatlipoca?"

The god's blue eyes flamed with rage, like twin shards of brimstone in the nethermost regions of Hell. Carol knew she was in great danger, but she couldn't stop. Her only chance for escape required she push this petty deity to his limits. "I wonder what sort of a people my ancestors would've been if they'd worshipped, say, Quetzalcoatl as their main god."

"Do not pronounce his name here, foolish girl." Huitzilopochtli's voice was cold and brittle. "His protection is meaningless in Mictlan. Besides, the feathery worm knows the truth: human life was stolen. *He stole it.* A price must be paid for it to continue. And his own temples flowed with the blood of sacrifice as well, lest you forget."

"I'm pretty sure that wasn't his idea."

Huitzilopochtli lifted his dart and pointed it at her menacingly. "You are too trusting of the worm and his mutt. But they cannot protect you. They cannot save your mother, either. You have mentioned Tezcatlipoca. In truth, he is a mighty force, one to which I bend my knee gladly. Under his aegis, I shall once again rule over humanity, and the blood of thousands will imbue my spirit with unimaginable might!"

His voice made her tremble, but she smirked as bravely as she could. "We won't let you. Me and Johnny. Xolotl. Quetzalcoatl. Tonantzin, the mother of all."

He simply stared at her, apoplectic. *Almost there.*

"Here I stand, the god of your ancestors, and you spit defiance at me. You are like Malintzín, turning your back on your people."

Carol knew he meant Malinalli Tenepal, the indigenous princess whose knowledge had helped Hernán Cortes defeat the Aztecs, the empire the young woman had blamed for the tragedies in her life. "They *weren't* her people. Her people had to pay *tribute* to the Mexica. She probably believed she was helping to free them. Her only mistake was thinking the Spaniards would be much better. Their view of the universe was also pretty messed up. I'll bet Tezcatlipoca had something to do with that, too. Didn't it ever occur to you that maybe he was pitting both sides against each other? He loves chaos and destruction, no? Wants to see the world end? Where do you fit in as god of humanity *if they're all dead?*"

Now. He'll hit me, throwing me toward his monster snake, and I'll get my chance. It'll hurt, but I'll heal quick.

Instead, Huitzilopochtli lowered his dart and nodded, his expression softening slightly. With a careless gesture, he let his shield tumble from his hand. It slapped against the black stone with a dull thud.

"I must admit, Carolina Garza," he said, his voice raspy with odd emotion, "that you indeed have a point. Truth be told, this conundrum is why I had you brought here. You understand, do you not, what the Dark Lord intends to do? He means to break you and your brother, to unhinge your minds or twist your wills so that you freely elect to place your *xoxal* into his hands. Bringing together his shadow sorcery and your savage magic, he will burst open the prison that contains the *Tzitzimime*, ancient star demons eager for your world's destruction."

Carol trembled, and not just at the frustration of her plan. Though she had basically figured out Tezcatlipoca's endgame, to hear it stated so matter-of-factly was frightening. Still, she clung to the shreds of her bravery, keeping her head high.

"We're not that easy to break."

The blue god's fist tightened around the dart as his free hand cut sharply through the acrid air. "He has broken emperors, philosophers, saints, *gods*. I assure you there is no other possible outcome if you continue along the Black Road."

"If we continue. As opposed to what, exactly?"

Huitzilopochtli reached out and touched her cheek. She felt a nervous surge within her, a burble of feelings she couldn't decipher. *Was that really me, or did he make that happen? Either way...Gross!*

"You ally with me. I can rally much of Mictlan under my banner, and together we can march against him and his boney puppets. Enemy of my enemy and so forth."

Carol felt absolutely no desire to join forces with the bloodthirsty deity. Nor did she believe for a second that he really wanted to overthrow Tezcatlipoca. *But if I play along some, maybe I can still make my plan work.*

"How can you expect me to trust you? I...I won't lie. It's been really hard, and I'm not sure we can make it to the center, much less take him on. But you...*You want to rule the world*. You say you need our help, but what happens after?"

"You can trust me," muttered the Aztec god of war, "because I am telling you the truth. Once we have defeated Tezcatlipoca, I shall demand your loyalty. And if you choose to defy my sovereignty, I shall kill you. Until then, however, we can work as...equals."

Yeah, right. "Prove it, then. Take your spell away so I can move around."

Huitzilopochtli shrugged and made a slight gesture with his right hand. "You have been released, but I caution you. Should you attempt to wield your savage magic against me, my fire serpents will rend you to bloody bits."

"You're a real charmer. Do all your potential allies get this treatment? Oh, yeah, I forgot. The Empire." She stretched and inched slightly toward Xiuhcoatl. "Okay, if we're really going to hash this out, I need Johnny here. I can't make a decision without him agreeing to it."

Nodding, the god lifted his head toward the gray sky. After a second or two, his eyes narrowed. "How odd."

"What?" Carol took another step to her left.

"I have called out to Tlecoatl, the serpent that has your sibling in its care, but it does not respond." He grew grim and bristled with cold ire. "For your sake, I hope..."

The Mexica god of war was unable to finish his sentence. Several things happened in very quick succession. A blue-green cloud hurtled down at Huitzilopochtli from above, surrounding him in a whirring blur that pulled at his cape and headdress, throwing him off-balance. Xiuhcoatl gave a roar of rage and leapt into the air. Carol threw herself to the ground, reaching her hand out and grasping the scale, setting her *tonal* free. Slipping from her clothes as her limbs retracted and reformed, she began to quickly grow in size. Deep in her belly fire rumbled hungrily, and her massive wings arched as they drew the acrid air downward, lifting her bulk above the black temple. Immediately she saw that the blue-green blur consisted of nearly a hundred hummingbirds, their needle-like beaks pricking repeatedly at the masked god.

Carol, it's me!

Which one?

ALL of them! Hurry, while I've got him freaked out.

Xiuhcoatl dove toward the cloud of birds, fire trembling in its jaws. Carol lashed out with the lower half of her body, striking the other serpent and sending it spinning toward Huitzilopochtli, spraying flame and smoke in haphazard spirals. The hummingbirds ripped the black cape away right before Xiuhcoatl struck his master full on, catapulting the god off the temple. Enraged, the serpent recovered and swooped toward the figure now hurtling toward the river of lava.

Huitzilopochtli stretched out his arms and halted mid-fall. Xiuhcoatl ducked below him, and the god of war straddled the flying serpent like a steed. Together they focused on the charm of hummingbirds, their fire and dark energy building with a groaning thrum that Carol could feel in her very bones. The feathered bits of Johnny flew together at the top of the temple, coalescing into the twelve-year-old boy, who wore the stolen cape draped around his unclothed body. Stooping quickly, he grabbed Huitzilopochtli's shield and, remaining in a crouch, lifted it before him just as a blast of flame and blue energy hit.

Johnny! Her fear for her brother's life and her rage surged within her. Her *tonal*, eager to release the fire that burned in her gut, hungrily soaked up the savage magic that her emotions tapped. As a white-hot stream blazed from her impervious jaws, she saw that the obsidian mirror at the center of the shield was reflecting most of the attack, hurling it back at Huitzilopochtli. Her fire and the ricochet merged and slammed into the god of war and his serpent, shoving them violently into the stream of lava below.

"Carol!" Johnny screamed, standing. "Let's get the hell out of here, quick!"

He gripped the black cape tightly about him and transformed, becoming an enormous harpy eagle. The cape melted into his morphed flesh. With razor sharp talons he scooped up the shield and took to the gray, ash-filled sky.

That was much better than the lechuza, huh? I think I figured out the clothes trick. Good thing, too. That other snake burned mine up.

Carol dipped her tail down, curled the tip around her own clothes, shoes and water jug, and followed him out of the caldera.

How did you get free?

I grabbed the little feather and figured I'd shift into a small bird, get away. But like halfway through the transformation my tonal kind of refused to go smaller, like maybe there's a limit or something. I was panicking, but the idea of a whole flock of birds popped into my head, and I guess I used xoxal *to make it happen.*

Carol did a barrel-roll to avoid a plume of ash lifting from a crater below. *Does it feel weird?*

What, being spread across a hundred little brains? Uh, yeah. But kinda cool, too. All these little parts of me that I'm not normally aware of? They got to work together. You'll have to try it. But maybe not when you're being pursued by a dragon-thingy. I tried to keep my clothes draped across a bunch of hummingbirds, but it blew fire on us, on me, I mean, and that was that. But I could maneuver better. I led it to a field of, like, steam geysers. Eventually one erupted right in our flight path. I managed to get out of the way, but the snake got barbecued.

Well, thank God you showed up when you did.

That was an Aztec demon?

God. Huitzilopochtli. He was trying to convince me that we needed to join up with him and overthrow Tezcatlipoca...and then install him as ruler of humanity.

Uh, megalomaniac much?

Right? But, uh, like the doppelgangers, his real purpose was to get me scared, I think. Make me doubt myself, doubt our ability to rescue Mom.

Heh. The moron basically gave us two more weapons to use. This cape is really powerful, Carol. I think Huitzi-whatever was a nagual, too. And his shield...You saw how it deflected all that power.

Yes, but, Johnny, those belonged to a man who became a god using cehualli. I don't think you can trust the shield or the cape. Promise me that the minute you sense something wrong, you'll get rid of them.

Waves of reassurance came from her brother. *Of course, sis. But I think I can handle them fine.*

Still, Carol worried as her massive wings rode the hot wind. What if the point of this desert had been to put those weapons in her brother's hands? She'd have to keep careful watch. Johnny had a habit of overestimating his own abilities. Since he was good at nearly everything he tried, he was never really prepared for the times when he sucked at something, and he would sometimes end up over his head in trouble as a result.

Carol's concern took a backseat as the beating of dozens of massive wings came from all around them. A group of fire-breathing flying serpents was converging on them, presumably furious at what the twins had done to their master. Johnny turned and flew backwards, raising the shield with his talons to deflect their flaming attacks. Carol ducked and weaved as she flew, narrowly avoiding streams of fire. When a wyrm would get too close, she'd blast it from the sky with her *xoxal*-enhanced blaze.

In this way the twins were chased through yellow, sulfuric clouds and mists of cooling steam. Below them, the lava fields and geysers gradually gave way to a vast, ashen plain. The wyrms gave a final shriek of rage and turned aside.

Five deserts down. Four more to go.

CHAPTER FOURTEEN

ohnny lowered himself to the ash-covered ground and shifted back into his human form. As he did so, he envisioned the black eaglet-down cape morphing into shirt, pants and shoes; the same as before when he'd absorbed it into the skin of his harpy eagle form. His savage magic manipulated the physical properties of the leather and feather garment, and soon he was fully clothed. Picking up the stolen shield, he slipped his arm through the inner strap and slung it over his shoulder.

The legless dragon that settled down beside him gave an annoyed grunt.

"Yeah, I know. I rock, huh?" Carol gestured with her huge, reptilian head. "What? Oh, turn around? Got it."

He gave her his back and looked around at the emptiness. White ash covered a completely flat plain as far as the eye could see. He noticed the ash had already begun to chalk up the black books he had materialized from the cape.

"Maybe you shouldn't have chosen black," his sister said. He turned in time to see her hopping on one foot as she struggled to pull on her shoes.

"Yeah, well, I'm learning as I go along. It's like, I don't know, harnessing lightning. The power's inside us, but we're pretty clueless about how to use it. Seems like need and desperation are the keys, though."

"Ah, you were desperately in need of *not* running around butt-naked through the Underworld," Carol quipped with a smile.

"Exactly. So, okay, ash. I would say that it doesn't seem like that big a deal, but, yeah, there's probably a catch that Big Red forgot to mention. So let's check. I've got the cape and the shield, but I lost my water. You still have yours, right?"

Carol patted the corked clay jug dangling from a belt loop. "Yeah. And the bag of jewels is still in my pocket. Since when are you Mr. let's-get-organized? I swear, give a boy a little savage magic and he starts acting like he's in charge."

"Oh, pardon me, boss. Should we start walking, ma'am?"

Carol rolled her eyes. "Come on, smart-alec."

As they trudged across the barren landscape, Carol explained in more detail what had transpired on the obsidian pyramid.

"Wow, okay. So human sacrifice. That's how he got his mojo."

Carol nodded, swallowing heavily. "Pretty twisted. All those innocent victims."

"Well, I don't know, Carol. Didn't our social studies teacher tell us last year that most of the people who got sacrificed wanted it? Volunteered or whatever?"

The look of disgust on his sister's face was predictable. She tended to get on a moral high horse about certain subjects, and getting her to see alternative perspectives was pretty hard. "The ones that volunteered were brainwashed by their priests and leaders. And most of the *volunteers* were captives, taken during the Flower Wars."

"Right. They were warriors. They figured dying that way was honorable, no?"

"They were dying for a *lie*, Johnny," Carol spat back. "The sun would've kept shining without their deaths. The universe wouldn't have come to an end."

"Maybe, maybe not. I've seen some weird stuff down here that makes me, you know, not want to assume *anything* anymore."

She looked at him like he was insane. "They sacrificed *children*, too. Look, the one thing we know for sure? Human sacrifice generates *cehualli*. I've been attacked by that shadow sorcery, and it's evil. Ergo, those traditions were wrong."

"Look, I agree with what you're saying, basically. I just don't want you to blame our ancestors or to make them out to be all bad."

Carol softened a bit. "No, of course not. The Aztecs were a great people. In terms of culture, science and guts, I admire them. Now that I know their gods actually *exist*, I definitely can't blame them for doing whatever they could to appease the dark ones. No, I am angry at the gods themselves, Johnny. They're the bad guys here."

"So, speaking of dark gods and stuff...Were you tempted? Even a little bit? I mean, in the movies you always see chicks falling for the old, powerful supernatural guys. You know, vampires and stuff."

"No way. That's just gross. He's like two thousand years old, Johnny." Her expression went thoughtful for a second. "And besides, he wasn't even cute or anything."

Johnny laughed. "I hope Tezcatlipoca's not listening in. All he needs to do is send some hot-looking demon, huh?"

"Shut up. That's stupid." She smiled at him as she gave him a little shove. "I'm barely going to be an eighth-grader. I don't even think about stuff like that."

"Uh-huh."

They joked at each other's expense while they followed the Black Road, barely visible beneath the ash. Soon they were stained to the knees with the white powder. Johnny was reminded of some of the empty lots between their house and Veterans Middle School, where semi-trucks parked sometimes, waiting to load or unload at a nearby warehouse. He'd run through those dusty, barren plots of land several times, trying to avoid a fight with some wannabe gangster. His father didn't approve of fights. *If someone picks on you or makes your life difficult, tell your teachers. Tell the principal.* Of course, what Dr. Garza didn't seem to realize was that the teachers didn't want to get involved, and the principal was just collecting a paycheck. Some days it seemed there was virtually no discipline. A series of food fights in April had even led to the arrival of a bunch of extra administrators from central office to keep an eye on the kids for a few weeks.

The upshot of the chaotic atmosphere was that Johnny had been forced to defend himself or Carol a couple of times. Not from any really dangerous people, just low-level punks looking to pick on the smart kids. Johnny, who like Carol was tall for his age, had gotten into three or four scrapes in sixth grade, and last fall he'd been in an actual knock-down brawl after school. He'd explained away the occasional bruise to his parents as the result of overly vigorous PE activities, and Carol, though she did not approve of these fights, had said nothing.

Now, of course, Mickey Mouse Maldonado would spend the summer thinking of ways to get back at Johnny for the humiliation of their last encounter. *He's got a surprise coming, Johnny mused with satisfaction. After tangling with a bunch of gods and monsters in the bowels of the Underworld, I'm not all that scared of his macho gangster crap.* He envisioned all the bullies he could put in their places with his new abilities, all the innocent kids he could defend. *Maybe I can even bring this shield out of Mictlan with me. Be sort of like, I don't know, the Hispanic Captain America. Or something.*

He entertained himself for what felt like hours, daydreaming about all the perks of being a *nagual*. From time to time Carol would break the silence with a question, but for the most part they didn't talk. The comfortable habit of shared reflection was an easy one to fall back on, and Johnny's heart warmed at the memory of many long summer days spent in each other's company, reading or writing or building stuff with Legos.

Gradually the twins began to perceive clouds of ash puffing skyward along the horizon. Harsh, grinding, almost mechanical sounds reached them across the desolate plain.

"I'm pretty sure that's not a train," Johnny quipped.

"Probably something bad. Things have been too calm for too long."

Johnny smiled. An eagerness to face the obstacle rose in him. *Danger is addictive. That's what Dad used to say. Well, he's right.*

"Let's check it out, then."

They picked up the pace, and before long they saw it: a monstrous creature with skin like cracked clay through which a red inner fire flickered. Its elongated head was topped by long, thin metal spikes that ran down its nape and along its spine.

Humanoid arms and legs were tipped in claws of the same material. As it glimpsed them, the thing opened its mouth wide, and from between iron teeth it belched an enormous cloud of white ash in their direction. The twins stopped in their tracks, but the powdery flakes settled on them like fresh snow.

"Whoa." Johnny smirked, brushing ash from his lips. "You really showed us, huh? Your scary ash is the last straw. We give up."

Carol muttered something under her breath. Johnny just ignored her. *She wouldn't know a good joke if it smacked her upside the head.*

The monster gave a dark, rumbling laugh. "Oh, delicious irony," it grated. "Continue. Share more of your sardonic quips, skinwalker."

"Why? Are you going to sing *'I'm rubber, you're glue— whatever you say bounces off of me and sticks to you'*? Wow, the Lord of the Dead really needs to hire some new thugs."

"Interesting you should mention substances that stick to one. You've not been a skinwalker long, have you, boy?"

Johnny turned to Carol. "You know what? Screw this talkative demon. Let's just shift and fly out of range of his stupid voice."

Not waiting for a reply, Johnny tried to release control to his *tonal*. But nothing happened. He couldn't even sense his shadow soul. In its place was...nothing.

"What the...?"

Carol had a look of confusion on her face. "I can't shift, Johnny."

"Yeah, neither can I."

"White ash, you imbeciles," the clay-skinned creature mocked. "The primary weakness of skinwalkers. You're both covered in it. You cannot slip your skin. And if something coated in the ash were to pierce your flesh—say, one of my tines—your blood would rush it to your heart, which would stop for all eternity."

His heart jolting in his chest painfully, Johnny unslung the shield. "Carol, get behind me."

Chuckling, the demon took several creaking steps forward. Its inner flame blazed brighter through the cracks in its skin. "Ah, miserable knave, do you not understand that iron shatters obsidian? That was the greatest lesson of the Conquest, you runt. *Iron. Shatters. Obsidian.* Now you will die. Perhaps I may allow your dog of a sister to live so that when she is broken over our Dark Lord's knee she can weep that her twin succumbed to the smoking hand of Nextepehua, Prince of Ashes!"

And with that, Nextepehua hurled itself at them, iron claws slashing. Johnny spun away, trying to keep his sister behind him. The Prince of Ashes landed a tremendous blow on the shield. The supernatural weapon held, but the impact was too great for Johnny's twelve-year-old muscles and he went sprawling in the ash. Lifting the shield, he struggled to regain his feet, but Nextepehua rained blow after blow against him, and Johnny soon found himself ground into the ash, wincing at the pressure on his arms and chest as the demon leaned its weight against the shield. Its horrifying face drew closer to his, and it opened wide its maw. Iron teeth gave off glints of orange and red, illuminated redly by the creature's inner fire.

Johnny fought and twisted and grunted, but there was no

getting free. *Oh, my God! Xolotl! Someone! Help! I can't die! I can't leave Carol to face this by herself! NO!*

There was a second of silence as Nextepehua gloated. Then Johnny heard a soft sloshing, a sniffle, and the sound of his sister clearing her throat.

Amazingly, she began to sing.

Allá en la fuente
había un chorrito,
se hacía grandote
se hacía chiquito.
Estaba de mal humor —
pobre chorrito tenía calor.

Nextepehua craned his head to look at Carol. Johnny could only make out her right hand: she had uncorked the clay jug of water the Little People had given her.

"Shapeshifting's not the only magic we've got, you freak. Now get off my brother before I go all Dorothy on you."

The Prince of Ashes spat sparks. "I do not fear you, wench."

"Yeah, that's one of the advantages of being a girl. People are always underestimating you."

Johnny saw her hand go back and forth; and she began to swing the bottle repeatedly. Every splash was like acid on Nextepehua's skin. Its inner flame guttered. Its skin began to run like mud.

"Father!" Carol shouted, punctuating the first splattering of water. "Son! Holy Ghost! Tonantzin! Quetzalcoatl! Xolotl! Mom! Dad! Johnny! ME!"

With the last drops of the sacred water, the Nextepehua's

fire went out, and the demon collapsed into a runny pool of wet clay, covering Johnny and the shield. *Nasty. Crap, did I just get a piece of wet demon skin in my mouth?* He began wriggling himself free. Carol immediately bent and helped him dig his way out.

"That was freaking awesome, Carol!" he said as he pulled free of the demon's remains with a gross sucking sound. "Now if it had just screamed, 'I'm melting, I'm melting', it would've been a perfect rescue."

She shook her head at him. "You're one crazy boy. You almost died, Moron."

"Yeah, well, I've got my magic-song-singing sister at my back, so it's all good."

Carol waved his good humor away as she rolled her eyes. "I think it would be smart to get as far away from this ash as we can. We need to wash up. Ew, especially you. You've got muddy demon guts all over you."

"I know. *Awe*-some," he joked in a high-pitched voice. "So what's the next obstacle, do you remember?"

Carol tried brushing some of the ash from her clothes as they started walking.

"Um, *heart-eating demons*?"

"Whoa. Finally, something that'll like us for what's on the inside instead of our incredible good looks."

He flashed a smile at his sister, and they picked up the pace.

CHAPTER FIFTEEN

Despite Johnny's good humor, Carol was nervous. Along the horizon she could make out a line of black stretching off into the indistinct distance. As they drew closer, the ash gave way to hard-packed earth, the Black Road carving its somber way straight toward the heart of Mictlan. Gradually, the dark line became a massive wall whose impossible length was broken every dozen or so kilometers by embedded minarets, massive spires that Carol figured must serve as watch towers or forts.

"Oh, fun." Johnny's voice was flat, as if even his playfulness were sapped by the enormity of the construction. "I'm not sure I really want to see what's on the other side of that wall. I mean, that's some impressive architecture, but…"

"Yeah, I hear you."

They continued in awed silence as the wall loomed higher and higher. Soon they saw that the Black Road led right up to a pair of dauntingly huge gates wrought of some slate-colored metal and flanked by obsidian towers. Beside the towers perched a half-dozen winged humanoid creatures with the faces of women, some with hideous beaks, some feathered, others leathery. All of them were snarling.

"Harpies," Carol muttered.

"Aren't those from Greek mythology?"

"Well, yeah. But I guess if they're real they'd probably pop up in all mythologies."

"Ah, yeah. You're right. Don't much like us, huh?"

The twins stopped about a hundred yards away. The harpies howled and spat a rain of nasty-smelling saliva that pattered the sand in front of their feet.

Johnny glanced around, nodding absently. "So, uh, this is an insane question, but...how do we get in?"

As if in answer, the heavy gates began to groan open and a dozen wraiths swirled through the gap to materialize before the twins. Carol's mouth went dry as she scrutinized them. Gray, nearly mummified flesh stretched across their angular bones, and their eyes glowed like hot coals above ragged nostril holes and predatory teeth. They wore thick, brine-soaked leather armor across chests, forearms, and shins as well as bone helmets filigreed in copper with hideous designs. Each of them bore a club, fashioned of copper, wood or bone, along the lengths of which had been embedded shards of obsidian.

One of the undead warriors had a black stripe running horizontally across his eyes. He stepped closer and spoke in a raspy, guttural voice. "By order of the Ajalob, puissant Lords of Xibalba, dread capital of Mictlan, you are now captives of the city guard. Accompany us immediately, or we will drag your living bodies through the streets by force."

Johnny raised his hands in a gesture of surrender. "No problem. We were headed this way anyhow, and we could use a zombie escort."

Carol shot him a look. *Are you an idiot?* she thought at him. *Do you see those weapons?*

144

Calm down, sheesh. I just don't want them to think we're afraid of them.

I am afraid.

Well, duh, me, too. But they don't need to know that.

The Captain of the Guard made an impatient gesture, and the twins walked through the gates, herded by the other undead warriors. The vista that unfolded was one of densely packed gray buildings lining twisting side streets, punctuated by black spires and towering mansions. Gritty smog hung like a shroud over the metropolis, deepening the natural gloom of Mictlan. Swooping lazily through the haze or clinging to rooftops were vast murders of crows and wakes of vultures; the closest swiveled their heads hungrily at Carol and Johnny as the twins entered Xibalba.

Cutting a broad swath through the midst of the city, the Black Road became an ample avenue upon which these strange figures made their way to mysterious destinations. More of the gray-skinned undead shambled along the cobblestones, along with cloaked skeletons, headless monsters, assorted were-creatures and tall demigods of dark and deadly beauty. From time to time shadowy forms would flit by, too fast or insubstantial to be clearly perceived, and occasionally a carriage drawn by magic or gruesome beasts would shudder past.

"Whoa. Welcome to Emerald City's twisted sister, huh?" Johnny quipped, trying to shrug off the overwhelming strangeness. Carol doubted that his whistling in the dark would work this time. *There's no getting away from this place unscathed. There must be hundreds of thousands of monsters here.*

Led by the city guard, the twins made their way down that dark boulevard, their shapeshifting still blocked by the white ash that clung to their skin and clothes. Three rivers crossed their path, spanned by bridges built of human bone. In the first river, huge scorpions floated, fought or flailed their tails angrily against the black water. As Carol glanced at the roiling scene in horror, a dozen humanoid creatures with scales and gills erupted from beneath the surface, impaling a good number of scorpions with bone harpoons before diving back under the current, pulling their prey along with them.

"Oh, look," muttered Johnny. "Creatures from the Black Lagoon."

"You are too weird."

"Weird? Carol, are your eyes even open? My weirdness is like super average behavior compared to this wack place."

Johnny had less to say as they crossed over the second river, a sluggish stream of red from which rose a faint warmth and with it a sickly stench. Gnats and flies and other vermin buzzed on its crimson surface. *Blood. There is a river of blood under my feet.* Carol bit back the urge to scream. The final bridge spanned an even more disgusting flow: a rank-smelling, brown-colored tributary upon the surface of which floated clots of rancid pus teeming with maggots. Carol retched, acid burning at her throat.

I'm going to be sick, she thought at her brother.

Just try to hold it down. They want to gross us out. It'd make them real happy to see our weakness.

After the rivers the avenue widened, expanding into strange parks in which dark, moss-festooned trees loomed obliquely over granite benches and sulfur-rich fountains. In the distance, an enormous shadowy shape began to coalesce. After a few minutes, Carol realized it was a huge ziggurat, one that dwarfed

Huitzilopochtli's temple. At its base stood a palatial structure with wickedly sharp arches and pillars in the shape of serpents twined around dying women. When they reached the base of the steps that led up to the building's shadowy portico, the Captain of the Guard stopped them.

"You are ignorant living children, so I will instruct you as to proper etiquette. This is the *Mitnal*, the Council Chamber of the Ajalob. As you enter the presence of the Thirteen, you will prostrate yourselves in obeisance."

Johnny cocked his head. "Uh, what?"

Carol touched his arm gently. "They want us to lie down on the floor to show our respect."

"Dude, I know what it means. He's just crazy if he thinks I'm going to kiss their bony asses like that."

The undead warrior scoffed harshly. "If you do not show the proper deference, knave, you will be obligated to do so. Once satisfied with your groveling, High Lord Kisin will bid you stand. At that point, the audience will begin. You are to remain still throughout. We will escort you out again once judgment has been passed."

"Wait, *judgment*?" Carol blanched. "Do you mean that this is a trial?"

"Of course it is, wench. You are living humans, trespassing in Mictlan, standing on the very Avenue of the Dead in Xibalba. Your violations of the Dark Lord's decrees carry a weighty price."

Our hearts, Johnny's voice echoed in her mind. *They're going to rip out our hearts.*

The Little People said we'd be okay. We swallowed the jade.

I'm not feeling real confident about the jade right now, Dude.

Prompted by the deadly clubs, the twins ascended the steps, crossed the portico and stepped through two copper-plated doors into a large chamber dominated by an elevated dais. It was furnished with a curved granite fixture that reminded Carol of the bench the Supreme Court sat at. Ringing the base of the dais stood six armored were-creatures with differing features. They were mainly hominoid but with the animal characteristics of a crocodile, stag, wolf, ape, jaguar and vulture. Each clasped a huge obsidian-tipped spear. Before them, in an oval depression that separated the platform from the rest of the chamber, a red-robed and hooded figure lifted a bony claw and announced in a gravelly voice:

"Abase yourselves before the Lords of the Black Quarter: Ah Pukuh, Hunhau and Akan."

The guards pushed on Carol's shoulders till she knelt. From the shadows behind the dais emerged three tall, gaunt figures garbed in black feathers and adorned with obsidian jewelry. Their faces were skulls that protruded through rotting, peeling flesh. Their eyes glowed a deep, unnatural blue. The trio took their places, folding themselves into high-backed thrones toward the middle of the bench.

"Tremble before the Lords of the Red Quarter: Yoaltecuhtli, Yoalcíhuatl and Tzontémoc."

Another three beings stepped from the shadows. They wore no robes or capes; instead, exposed muscle and meat glistened red and slick, as if the skin had been flayed away. Wreaths of fire encircled their bloody heads, and their eyes were like burning coals. They took up positions near the Lords of the Black Quarter, leaving a single throne between the two groups.

Okay. I am officially freaking out, she thought at Johnny, her heart beating madly.

Just pretend it's a real gory horror flick.

I hate horror.

Oh, that's right. Crap.

"Look on the Lords of the White Quarter and know despair: Techlotl, Cuezalli, and Itzcoliuhqui."

Pale, corpse-like demons wrapped in shrouds floated across the dais. Dazzling white tongues of fire danced above their heads. Their eye sockets were empty, but the blackness within bored into Carol as they arranged themselves at the far left edge of the bench.

They can see into me, she realized. *They know my weaknesses.*

"Lastly, the Lords of the Green Quarter, sickly sweet and source of rot: Chalmécatl, Chalmecacíhuatl, and Nexoxocho."

The trio that appeared next were rotting corpses whose moldy flesh was covered by moss, toadstools, and strange lichens. Bright, poisonous flowers encircled their foreheads and their bodies teemed with beetles, worms and flies. Snakes wriggled out of their mouths and into their eye sockets as they took up spots at the far right end of the dais.

Okay, now even I am grossed out. Johnny winked at her.

"Now, prostrate yourselves, humans, before the Chief of this Council, Speaker of the Ajalob, High Lord Kisin."

A very tall and very thin man strode slowly from the darkness. His dark skin clung tightly to his skull, and his lank black hair spilled down his back. He was dressed in what appeared to be elegant Spanish clothing from the 16th century: a white silk shirt, black velvet doublet and breeches, and blood-red leather boots and jerkin that Carol suddenly suspected were made of human skin. As Kisin lowered his dark brown eyes upon the twins, Carol slumped face-first onto the floor, her arms outstretched. Beside her, Johnny did the same.

That jerk used magic to make me go all prostrate! Son of a...

Stop, Johnny. Let him have his fun. Remember what we're here for. We need to get past them and get Mom.

"Twins. Once more." Kisin's voice was smooth and rich, but also cold and haughty. *The voice of a sociopath.* "How I tire of twins. Nonetheless. As living beings you have trespassed in both Mictlan and its capital city, Xibalba. You have thereby violated the natural order established by the Dark One and your own feathered worm. You have, further, ignored edicts decreed by Lord and Lady Death by traveling the Black Road and using force against its guardians. Have you aught to say in your defense, urchins?"

Johnny pushed himself up, regarding High Lord Kisin with anger and disgust. "If being alive in Mictlan is a violation of the natural order, then Tezcat did it first. He brought our mom to this stupid place. And I'm pretty sure he wanted us to come looking for her. So, yeah, this is jacked up. Stop pretending like you freaks have justice down here, and let's move on to the sentencing, 'kay?"

Though Carol was frightened out of her wits, she felt a surge of pride in her brother. She wanted to applaud or hug him. Kisin's power, of course, held her firmly in place.

The High Lord grimaced and gestured dismissively. Johnny's face slammed against the cold stone floor with a crunching thud. "Very well. Juan Ángel and Carolina Garza, the Ajalob declare you guilty to your hypocritical cores. You are sentenced to die upon the Great Temple of Tezcatlipoca at the end of two more watches: sixteen of your living hours. Once your young hearts have been ripped from your chests, we will feast on them. Then your shades will wend their fleshless way to annihilation at the center of Mictlan."

Two guards seized them by the shoulders and yanked them to their feet.

"In the interim, you are remanded to the *cuauhcalli* to await the ceremony that will end your meaningless lives." Kisin turned his back on them and faded into the darkness. The other lords stood as one and floated backward into the shadows as well.

T he *cuauhcualli* was a sort of stone dungeon beneath the *Mitnal*. Carol sat on the cold floor of their cell, scrubbing at the ash with her hands, trying to dust enough of it off to access her tonal. She believed that the Little People hadn't lied and that somehow the jade could protect them from being sacrificed, but she didn't want to depend solely on that. *It would be really good if we could shift and fly the heck out of here.*

Johnny simply leaned back against the rough wall, tapping out a beat against his stolen shield with his fingers and humming some of that weird techno music he loved so much. His dark hair spiked out in all directions, and the ash on his skin made him appear almost ghost-like. The black clothes he'd formed from Huitzilopochtli's cape had turned nearly gray with the dust. *I must look just as bad. Gah. I really need a bath. Don't suppose they have water around here, though.* She thought about the nasty rivers they'd crossed and gave a little shudder.

A clanging sound broke the relative silence, and their dog-headed guard peered at them through the bronze bars of the cell door. "You've a visitor, maggots. And she's a goddess, so keep your distance and know your place."

The door swung open at his touch and a short, dark woman swept into the cell. She wore a red cotton skirt and *huipil*, a sleeveless blouse, both items decorated with black crescent moons. The hem of her skirt was spattered with mud and what smelled like excrement, a mixture that smeared her bare feet and calves as well. Her long, black hair was swept back in a braid and atop her head sat a strange conical hat with white cotton tassels. Under expressive brown eyes, her broad nose was pierced by a crescent moon shaped ornament fashioned of bone. A triangle of black spread its way across her mouth to end under her chin. In her right hand, she carried a rustic, ancient broom.

"Whoa," Johnny muttered, "an Aztec witch."

The goddess leaned forward, sniffing at him. "Ah, the smell of early puberty. You will have need of me later in life, little man. You will discover both sides of my nature. But to respond, no, I am not one of your European witches. The broom is for sweeping away filth, disease, and sadness and the hat is a gift from my beautiful Huasteca people, crafted nearly three millennia ago. I am Ixcuinan, the Paradox, Queen of Sin and Forgiveness."

Carol nodded. She recognized their visitor now. She had read about her in one of her father's books. "They also call you Tlazolteotl, don't they? Goddess of the life cycle."

Ixcuinan reached out her hand and patted Carol on the cheek. A warm, sisterly feeling spread throughout her soul. "Indeed. I embody living movement, from the moment of your birth to the final confession you make before death, and all the earnest attempts at happiness in between. I urge you toward sin, but only so far. Just enough to know its taste. Then I devour it for you, allowing you to cleanly pass Beyond."

"Ah, that explains the *chapopote* on your chin." Johnny didn't seem impressed by the presence of the goddess. *Typical guy.*

"Yes," Ixcuinan replied, unperturbed. "One day, if your soul chooses this route upon your death, your sin will stain my mouth as well, Juan Ángel Garza. I suspect you will be less dismissive then. In any event, I have not come to sing my own praises. I am here to offer you aid."

Carol's eyes widened. "Why would you help us?"

Ixcuinan's free hand went to her dangling silver earrings, making them jingle musically. "There are many residents of Xibalba who resent Tezcatlipoca's heavy-handed usurpation of Mictlan. It is true he established this place here at the root of the World Tree, but its governance was placed in the hands of Lord and Lady Death. His interference runs counter to the natural order. I understand how frightening we must seem to you, but for thousands of years there was a discernible, noble purpose to our existence. As balance incarnate, I am disgusted by the Dark One's goal of universal destruction. He would like nothing better than for you two to be trapped in Xibalba, driven to despair by your inability to save your mother. Then would you either misuse your *xoxal*, splitting the World Tree and freeing the *Tzitzimime* to wreak havoc on the cosmos, or surrender that savage magic unto Tezcatlipoca's hand, thereby ensuring the same end. No, you must leave this city, and quickly, too. We are few, those who dare flout his authority, but powerful. Gods of vice and excess, for the most part, like the Ahuiateteo, who would be nothing should humans cease to exist."

Johnny smirked. "Great. Our new allies are the drunken junkie gods."

Ixcuinan laughed warmly. "Oh, I believe they will enjoy that label. Clever boy. Do not discount our abilities, however. We will come for you soon and escort you to the next level of your journey. Till then, rest unburdened."

She swept her broom in an arc that passed over both their hearts. Instantly, Carol felt refreshed and energized, as if a great weight had been lifted from her soul. Before she could speak her thanks the door swung open and the guard spoke brusquely. "Lady Ixcuinan, your pardon, but your time with the humans is at an end."

The goddess smiled, her teeth gleaming white against the stain of sin. For a moment, her features blurred and an older, wizened face seemed to shine from behind her flesh. Then she spun about, her braid whistling through the air, and hurried from the cell.

Several hours later, rescue had still not come. Johnny raised his eyebrows pointedly, nodding at the cell door.

"Uh, looks like the drunken junkie gods are too high to save us. Figures."

Carol sighed. "I'm sure they just got delayed or something."

"Maybe. Or maybe the Ish-Queen was doing Tezcat's will, faking us out, making us freak even more."

Carol didn't want to believe that, but when the cell doors

opened to reveal the city guard, waiting to escort them to their deaths, she collapsed inwardly. *I guess I thought I saw something in her that wasn't there. The Virgin. Tonantzin. Some spirit of sisterhood that could make her my ally.*

From their cells the twins were led along a narrow tunnel that angled upward till it ended right at the temple's base. Thousands of were-creatures, demons and monsters thronged about the ziggurat, and as Carol and Johnny emerged, a roar of excitement went up that set the very ground to trembling.

"Hey, cool." Johnny smiled and winked. "We're famous. All the demons are cheering us."

"They're excited to see us sacrificed, Johnny."

"Yeah, but that's something, no?" He laughed and turned to the guards. "Famous, notorious…all the same, huh, guys?"

"Shut up and climb the stairs, human," the captain growled, wresting the shield from Johnny's grasp.

"Sheesh!" Her brother's hands shot into the air in an exaggerated gesture of exasperation. "I'm going, dude. Hello. My adoring fans await. Got to give them a *heart-felt* performance, no? All my Xibalban rivals will just *eat their hearts out*, seriously."

Carol rolled her eyes and groaned. *Is this really the time for your cheesy jokes? They're going to kill us!*

We won't die. You even said it—the Little People have our backs. I'm guessing the Lords of Nasty are going to yank out the pieces of jade.

Yeah, well, I've been thinking about that. Aren't they going to notice that those aren't our hearts? Won't they just, I don't know, reach back in and remove the real ones?

I think we just have to have faith, Carol. There's really nothing else we can do. If Quetzalcoatl or God or whoever wants us to get Mom and defeat Tezcat, they're going to have to step up and protect us. I'm done worrying.

The guards prodded them roughly, and Carol began to climb. The steps were steep and slick, but thankfully the pyramid's sides were slanted at a relatively comfortable angle. Nonetheless, after finishing the first set of steps, standing on a broad stone landing upon which the second level of the ziggurat had been built, her leg muscles burned fiercely. By the time they'd reached the third such landing, Carol was out of breath, red-faced, and sweating like mad.

Panting, Johnny gasped sarcastically, "Good workout, huh? Got to recommend it to my jock friends. Oh, wait. I hate jocks. Now I'm *really* recommending it. Especially for the prize they get when they reach the top."

A guard shoved him toward the last flight of steps. Carol followed quickly, not wanting any more prodding from those painful clubs. She kept her eyes down, focusing on her aching feet, postponing the need to look up at the temple proper. Finally, though, she reached the top and had to take in the tableau. The cube-shaped temple sported a large obsidian mirror which faced her. Immediately in front of it was a huge stone receptacle in the shape of a jaguar, its back hollowed out to receive, she imagined, the hearts of sacrificial victims. Between that basin and the twins rose the altar, a massive slab of granite, mottled with stains that were certainly old blood.

"Whew! Two hundred and sixty freaking steps!" Johnny stretched, his joints popping. "I see you've got my bed ready. Perfect. I am *super* tired."

Arranged on either side of the temple were the Ajalob; the red and green lords to Carol's left, the black and white to her right. From within the temple, High Lord Kisin emerged. He now wore a black robe that reached his bare feet. His face was painted black, and a black powder that smelled to Carol's heightened senses like crushed scorpions and spiders had been rubbed into his forearms and neck. In his left hand he twirled a deadly looking obsidian blade.

"Indeed." His gaunt face spread in a wicked smile. "Then do climb right up, living boy, and rest a while."

Johnny shrugged, but Carol could hear his heart pounding as he approached the slab and pulled himself onto it. Immediately, a lord from each of the four quadrants of Xibalba moved forward and took hold of an arm or leg, immobilizing her brother. Kisin moved toward him, brandishing the blade. He began chanting in some dark, ancient tongue. A shadowy force gathered in the air like a silent oblivion, and smoke began to pour from the mirror, curling its way along the top of the pyramid, twisting around the altar's base.

"O, Tezcatlipoca, Lord of the Near and the Nigh, Night Wind, Enemy of Both Sides. Receive this life that we end for you, and may such a death herald many more, until a darkness pervades the living world and Mictlan erupts upon the Earth."

Carol felt her brother's thin courage falter as the knife blurred upward in the high lord's hand.

"Wait!" he cried, and his soul struck out wildly, despairing.

Carol could bear no more. Mustering all of her energy, she opened her mouth to sing, intending to send notes of pure *teotl* pounding against Kisin. The first quavering note had barely left her lips, when he shook his head and pointed his free hand at her, closing his fingers together in a gesture of silence.

"Enough of your twittering, little bird."

She found herself frozen in place, unable to move or speak as the black blade sliced through the air.

Don't look. Johnny's last thought flitted through her heart, but she couldn't avert her eyes. Kisin cut open her brother's chest, hacking through his shirt, and with a deft movement he plunged his hand inside and drew forth a pulsating red mass. He lifted it high into the air and was immediately rewarded by the raucous cheers of thousands of monsters in the streets below. Then, with a fiendish flourish the high lord tossed the heart into the hollow in the back of the stone jaguar.

The four lords released Johnny's limbs as he went limp. Kisin motioned to the guards. "Send this filth rolling down the steps. Let the Ahuiateteo and their ilk feast on his flesh."

The guards seized Johnny's body roughly and prepared to flip him over the edge. The Captain of the Guard, however, interrupted them. "Here. Set him on his shield and let's watch him rush at them willy-nilly."

Carol wanted to scream but her throat was locked. The undead soldiers dropped Johnny's unmoving form into the curve of the stolen shield and sent him rocketing down the steps of the ziggurat.

Kisin crooked his fingers at her, and against her will Carol moved toward the slab. With jerky movements, she climbed atop it and lay down, her brother's blood warm and sticky beneath her back. The four lords wrapped dead hands around her ankles and wrists as Kisin intoned his ancient chant. Sinking deeper into herself, Carol tried not to listen, tried not to see. The knife arced up through the gray sky, and she fled from consciousness before it could fall.

CHAPTER SIXTEEN

Emerging from a deep pool of nothing, Johnny felt water soak him from head to feet. Someone was drenching him.

Then he felt the pain. Sharp. Deep. Aching. His chest felt like someone had reached a hand in and...*Oh, yeah.*

"Wake up, little man. You must transform to heal yourself."

Johnny groaned. He just wanted to lie where he was, maybe sink back into oblivion away from the agony.

"You are extremely close to death, Juan Ángel. Shift. *Now.*"

He felt something stir within him, excited and unbridled at last. His *tonal,* free from the effects of white ash. Almost whining with a will to burst free from human form, it nudged at Johnny spiritually, urging him to step aside and cede control.

Johnny was happy to oblige.

With a powerful bound, the jaguar leapt to all fours, Huitzilopochtli's cape merging with its fur, crowding the black spots more densely. Johnny peered through its eyes at Ixcuinan, who was turning toward a body lying twisted and broken upon...

Wait. What's this stuff? We're on a huge pile of human bones! The uneven surface shifted beneath his paws as he moved closer to the goddess of filth and cleansing. The body she was kneeling beside came into focus.

It was Carol.

Johnny made a muffled sound somewhere between a cry and agonized wail and Ixcuinan reached back to caress his head gently between the ears. Her touch soothed him to the root of his tail. The goddess shifted her attention back to his sister, upending a large clay jar filled with clean water and washed the blood and ash away from Carol's face, neck and arms.

"Carolina," she muttered. "Come back to yourself. You must transform. You are badly injured, nearly dead. Find your *tonal*, daughter mine. Let it shape your broken flesh, heal your hurts."

She continued coaxing until Carol's body jerked and heaved, the wolf pushing its way through the girl and then freeing itself from her clothes.

Thank God, she thought at him weakly. *You're alive.*

Just barely. If it hadn't been for our friendly neighborhood witch here...I guess you were right, Sis.

Ixcuinan stood, regarding them both. "I cannot hear your communication, but I can imagine you wonder why I delayed in rescuing you. The truth is that this was always the plan and we could not risk revealing the details. Once High Lord Kisin removed your false hearts and sent your bodies tumbling down the pyramid, the Ahuiateteo spirited you away to this place, where the bones of the devoured are laid to rest and, for a time, the Ajalob will believe that we feast on your flesh. But when they take up the red jade for their own ugly nourishment, they will learn the truth. So we must hurry. There is no gate barring your way out of Xibalba. The Black Road runs unimpeded right across the border. There is nothing deeper in Mictlan we need to keep out."

Without another word, she turned and began to make her

way across the mountain of bone. Johnny bent his head to his amulet and bit lightly on the screech owl feather. In seconds he was scooping up his shield and Carol's clothes.

Good thinking. Carol wagged her tail briefly then set off after Ixcuinan. Johnny followed closely, his wings catching the noxious breeze that blew out of the city gates. As they made their way down the gentle slope of the ossified hill, Johnny relived the final moments before High Lord Kisin had slit him open. Though he had struggled to keep his cool, to stand up to the Ajalob as he had to many school bullies, in the end he had wanted to bolt and run. When that knife had begun its descent, he had felt for a moment the desire to agree to anything, to abandon this crazy quest, to help the dark forces tear down the foundations of the universe itself in order not to feel Kisin's hand reach inside him and wrench at his vital organs.

But I survived it. Both of us did. We faced one of the crappiest, scariest things anybody ever has, and we're okay.

The realization emboldened him. *Two more obstacles, and then we face ol' Tezcat himself,* he thought at Carol. *I think we're going do it.*

Yeah, how much worse can it get?

Right?

Ixcuinan and Carol reached the bottom, and Johnny landed beside them, shifting back into his human form and dressing himself with Huitzilopochtli's cape. He was perfectly healed, with just the faintest line of a scar across his diaphragm.

"You might want to switch to girl mode," he said, but the wolf shook her head. "Okay, suit yourself." He slung his shield over his shoulder and scooped up his sister's clothing and shoes, double-checking for the jewels.

Ixcuinan motioned for them to keep moving. They crossed a glittering plain of feldspar and finally reached the Black Road, which seemed to disappear a short distance away at the horizon.

"What did Xolotl say was next?" Johnny mused aloud.

Ixcuinan gave him a strange glance. "The hound assisted you?"

"Yeah. Didn't you get the memo? The Feathered Dude has got our back. Well, except for back there just now."

"Oh, Xolotl could have never passed the gates of Xibalba. Not without an army, and that is not Quetzalcoatl's way."

"That's what everybody keeps telling us." Johnny tried not to sound like a pouting child. "Anyway, he said that next we're going to face obsidian winds and a putrid lake. Doesn't sound too bad. But then, there were a bunch of things he failed to mention about the other deserts, so…Yeah."

Ixcuinan nodded. "He has indeed neglected to mention several complicating factors. For example, the air above Apan-huiayo makes flight…"

A sound like wind sweeping over loose gravel made them all spin around. A narrow swath of grass was weaving its way across the feldspar toward them, growing at a dizzying speed, tendrils reaching closer and closer. Across the path ran two figures, moving so fast they were almost a blur. The grass reached the edge of the Black Road and quickly twined upward into the air, forming a humanoid shape that stepped free of the verdant trail and faced Ixcuinan. The other two figures joined the humanoid. One was a tall, thin creature with black fur and the features of a hare, and the other looked like a were-lizard.

"The Swamp Thing, Frank from *Donnie Darko* and the Lizard

from *Spider-Man*," he couldn't help but blurting out. "You guys have *got* to be the drunken junkie gods, right?"

The hare-like god grinned. "To be sure, I am presently more sober than I would prefer, but we are indeed three of the Ahuiateteo." Turning to Ixcuinan, he dropped the smile and spoke more softly. "The Ajalob have discovered our deceit. They are furious. Our other brothers engaged them so we could warn you, but they cannot hold them long."

Ixcuinan gripped her broom tightly. "How soon?"

The grassy creature hissed. "They are on the Black Road, less than one thousand cuahuitls distant."

The reptilian god flicked its tongue at the air. "We will need all four of you, Lady."

Before Johnny could ask what that meant, Ixcuinan touched his shoulder and pointed her broom at the horizon.

"Juan Ángel, Carolina, you need to run as fast as you can to the edge of Xibalba. Neither the Ajalob nor the city guard can follow you into Itzeecayan, Land of the Cold Razor Winds. We will hold them off until you reach its border. Remember, Mictlan was not always a place of evil. I wish you success. Now go."

She hunched over, muttering mystically, then she suddenly stood, slamming the butt of her broomstick against the surface of the Black Road, once, then twice. Four women now stood in her place: a girl the same age as the twins, a young woman, a middle-aged matriarch, and an old, wizened crone. They glanced at the twins and screamed in unison.

"*GO!*"

Carol exploded into motion, her lupine form darting toward the horizon. Johnny bent his head and followed as fast as he could. When he found that he couldn't keep up, he half-shifted into a were-jaguar and quickly made up the distance between them. From behind him came sounds of battle: explosions, clanging weapons, cries of anger and pain.

The border's just ahead, Carol's voice muttered in his mind. *The Black Road narrows, and there's like a low wall on either side of an archway. No gate, like she said. Just a little toll booth or something on the left.*

They made a final dash for the exit. Two sentries rushed from the guardhouse onto the road, obsidian-tipped spears at the ready, ember eyes narrowing above their ragged nostrils. Carol leapt onto one, snarling as she tumbled him senseless to the ground. Johnny snapped the other's spear easily, clawing at his zombie face before passing under the arch and down a slope into the next desert.

He was first greeted by the sound of howling, shuddering winds that whipped across a stony plain, then by the blades. It was a small one first, shaving its way past his shoulder, taking a hunk of fur with it.

Johnny took a step back. "What the...?"

Then came larger shards, one of which slammed into his thigh before he pulled the shield off his shoulder, to crouch behind it for protection.

Carol, get behind me! These freaking winds are blowing razor-sharp hunks of rock everywhere!

He immediately felt her hot breath on his back as she took refuge. *Any ideas?*

Well, the Little People probably gave us something to deal with this, no? He looked down at his amulet. One of the two bits of animal matter that he hadn't tried was a thin, hollow tooth.

Crocodile, he realized, relying on his animal senses. *Thick skin. That's the answer.*

He let Carol know. She had also found something, a sickle-shaped claw that she believed belonged to a giant armadillo.

Awesome. We'll be slow, but we'll be armored.

After helping his sister arrange her clothes in a sling across her back, Johnny grabbed the tooth and shifted. It was an odd feeling, moving with short powerful legs that slung his belly so close to the rocky soil, and the reptilian instincts he had access to were very different from those of mammals and birds. But he was close to the ground, where the constant gale was less intense and fewer obsidian razors reached. With an awkward, deliberate gait, he began moving along the wind-eroded road. Carol followed close behind.

I don't know about you, he thought after a while, *but once through this wack place is enough for me. When I die, I'm going Beyond the Catholic way.*

Well, dork, considering all the sins you'll probably commit, I'm betting you'll spend a good, long time in Purgatory or whatever.

Nah, a lifetime of being your brother makes me automatically a candidate for sainthood.

Ha. Ha. Seriously, though...are you alright? The Ajalob were pretty brutal with you. I felt so bad that I couldn't help you.

Well, it was pretty lame, but...I think we had to go through it, you know? Face that horror. I'm betting what's got Mom is way worse.

Yeah, I, uh, kind of blacked out before they cut me, but they just hurled my body down the steps, not like your ride on a shield. When Ixcuinan coaxed me back...I don't even want to think about that pain.

Bad, huh?

That's pretty much an understatement. I don't know how I was able to focus long enough to shift. But I see where you're going with this. It's going to be ugly, isn't it? Saving Mom.

I think so, yeah.

Well, then it's a good thing this is taking forever, because I really needed a break.

Any of the blades hurt you yet?

Oh, I feel them, but they're not doing any damage.

Ditto here.

A comfortable pause came then as they trudged across the stony landscape. Johnny ran scenarios through his mind, the sorts of tricks he might need to try in order to get his mother free. Sitting in the Xibalban jail, he had found a single strand of black hair stuck in one of the feathers that fringed Huitzilopochtli's shield, and he'd carefully knotted it into place with his other of animal bits and DNA. He had no idea whether the idea at the back of his mind was feasible, and he really hoped that he wouldn't have to try it. *Insurance,* he told himself. *A backup in case nothing else works.*

Amazingly, the twins met up with no further obstacles as the terrain sloped ever downward. The horizon became a circular wall of rocky sand, sloping off in all directions. Looking straight ahead, Johnny could make out a thread of white descending directly opposite them. He glanced to the left and then to the right: red and green paths curved downward. *The other three roads.* They were nearing the center and bottom of Mictlan.

The winds whipped crazily around in circles for a few minutes, and then they were past Itzeecayan. The absence of the roaring gales was jarring, even for a crocodile's limited hearing.

Johnny shifted into a human again and looked around. The gloomy light from the eternally gray sky was reduced even more by the sloping land all about them. Looking toward the center of the Underworld, Johnny saw another body of water, broad and still like a lake, curving annular around the heart of Mictlan, shrouded in thick mists just a few kilometers away.

"I'm back to girl shape or whatever you called it," Carol said behind him. "Are we there yet?"

Johnny smiled as he looked back at her. "Remember how irritated Dad would get when you would ask that?"

She laughed. "Yeah. But the cool thing was that he always answered, even though he sounded frustrated. I don't remember him ever telling me to shut up."

Johnny nodded. "He's a pretty good guy. But he needs his wife, and we need our mom. So let's go get her, what do you say?"

"Órale," Carol responded, in perfect imitation of their mother.

They soon began to notice a strange smell similar to rotten eggs. The odor grew stronger as they approached the body of water, till it was nearly overpowering. Standing at its edge it looked to be a fetid mix of decomposing flesh, foul waste and acrid minerals. The air was thick and soupy and very likely poisonous. *We've got to get through this quick.*

Across the impenetrably black waters stretched a narrow stone bridge with no railings or other protection. It simply hung there in defiance of all laws of gravity, daring the twins to attempt a crossing.

"Well, I'm not swimming through that disgusting crap, so the bridge it is," Johnny announced.

Carol took a ragged breath through her mouth, probably trying desperately not to let the air filter into her nose. "Or we could just fly, hello."

Johnny nearly face-palmed at his own stupidity. "Of course. Lechuza time!"

Shifting into a screech owl, he grasped his shield in his talons and took flight, figuring Carol would follow him shortly. His wings beat the air above the noxious lake, but he felt himself being sucked down instead of going up. He struggled to gain altitude, but the air seemed to actively force him toward the inky water.

"Johnny!" his sister screamed as the shield actually slapped the surface. *Oh, crap!* He dredged up as much *xoxal* as his fear would let him, and in an exhausting burst of energy, he managed to flap his way to the stone causeway, tumbling into his twelve-year-old human form and panting heavily as he tottered to his feet. The bridge was only a meter wide at best, and Johnny was sorely tempted to stretch his arms out on either side to maintain his balance.

"Can't fly!" he called to his sister. "I think that's what the goddess was about to tell us before she split into four and started kicking demon butt. Looks like we're walking, Sis!"

She stopped fiddling with her necklace and walked carefully toward him. "I feel like gagging," she muttered as she approached.

"Right? I guess we know where the Mictlandians drain their sewers, huh?"

"Mictlandians? I don't think that's what they're called."

"Yeah, well, 'inhabitants of Mictlan', just doesn't have the same ring to it, and I guess they're not exactly *demons* since this isn't Hell."

Carol shrugged. "Whatever. You're just weird, in my honest opinion."

They continued making their careful way across the thin strip of stone, doing their best not to faint at the stench, which got impossibly worse as they neared the center. Johnny's eyes began to water and his nose to run. His very skin felt like it was breaking out in a rash.

"This is super unhealthy," he croaked. "But at least my sinuses are clear now."

Carol didn't reply; she just scuffled along behind him, her hands on his shoulders.

They reached what Johnny judged was the midpoint when the attack came. A half-dozen winged creatures that looked like gargoyles seemed to materialize out of thin air, diving toward the bridge, mouths open to utter sepulchral cries. One of them slammed into Johnny, knocking him into the tarry waters. He landed on his back, and the shield kept him afloat momentarily as he watched the winged monsters harry his sister, who had knelt and was feverishly flipping through options on her necklace.

The sluggish currents of the Apanhuiayo, as Ixcuinan had called it, sucked at him, and he knew that there was no way he would be able to swim the rest of the way. He considered his bracelet for a moment. Only one bit of animal matter was left to try, a clump of fur that reminded him of a seal's slick body.

Here goes nothing, he thought, and let his *tonal* leap into action. Water that had threatened to drown him instantly felt friendly and navigable. Four powerful legs ending in webbed, simian hands plied the inky sludge easily, aided by an agile tail tipped, inexplicably, with a fifth hand. Setting aside questions,

Johnny rocketed toward the inner shore, praying that Carol had found a solution to her dilemma.

As if in answer, the air all around exploded into flame. Johnny's ears were greeted by the screams of fricasseed gargoyles and a dragon's roar of triumph.

Ah, you shifted into the fire serpent. Smart move.

Yes, well, the bridge can't handle my weight, so I'm going to have to race you as it collapses behind me!

Very cinematic.

Dork.

He could hear chunks of the causeway fall into the lake with muffled splashes, generating waves that pushed him even more quickly to shore. He turned and saw Carol leap the last ten meters or so, landing heavily on the ground near him.

Johnny shook the last of the putrid water from his slick fur and morphed back into human shape.

"I don't know *what* the hell that was," he said, checking his shield as he gave Carol his back. "But thank God the Little People included it."

"I'm pretty sure it was a water dog a, what's it called, an *ahuizotl*. Read about them in one of Dad's reference books on Mexican legends. Wait, don't turn around yet."

Having confirmed that Huitzilopochtli's shield was still intact, Johnny looked ahead. The mist was very similar to what they'd seen upon entering the land of the dead and what had shrouded the desert of silence. Thinking of what might lie beyond it made his heart lurch with fear. *Let's keep that feeling to ourselves, okay,* tonal? *Carol needs her brother's courage right now. I'm betting real darkness is on the other side.*

170

Carol touched his arm, and he turned to look at her. Her clothes were scorched and ripped, her hair a total mess. But her eyes burned with a fierceness he recognized well: it was their mother's determined, almost obstinate spirit.

"Well, here we are at last, Johnny. We crossed the Nine Deadly Deserts, faced everything they could throw at us, and here we are at the center of Mictlan. Ready to face the Grim Reaper and his beautiful bride Catrina?"

Johnny nodded. "Ready as I'll ever be, Sis."

He took her hand, and they stepped through the veil.

CHAPTER SEVENTEEN

Carol scrunched her eyes tightly closed as they moved through the mist. The ambient sounds changed radically as they passed into the heart of Mictlan: it sounded like they were now outdoors in some corner of the human world with wide spacious skies above them. She opened her eyes and was greeted not with the absolute darkness she had feared but with an amazing otherworldly landscape. Above them, seemingly hundreds of meters away, the impossibly thick roots arched through the sky, as if Mictlan lay beneath some cosmic tree. Between the roots peeked trillions of gorgeous stars, their ancient light illuminating her surroundings more than the gloomy gray of the nine deserts had ever done.

Before them, the mist-shielded core of Mictlan was dominated by a mind-boggling structure: a fortress formed of red crystal that jutted insanely this way and that in defiance of any human notion of symmetry or aesthetics. The complex sported twisted spires that nearly touched the roots above, and it sprawled for what seemed kilometers in all directions. The Black Road terminated at a vast opening that gaped like a hungry maw.

Carol's heart ached suddenly as it hadn't in some time.

"She's in there."

Johnny squeezed her hand and then let go. "Yeah. I can feel her, too. Let's go save her, no?"

As they began to move toward the fortress a huge parliament of owls fluttered out of its crevices to settle all around them, hemming them in. Huge *lechuzas* and smaller *tecolotes* cocked their heads silently and wouldn't move aside. When Johnny tried to push some out of the way with his foot, a group of them lifted into the air before him, hovering in silent menace, talons at the ready.

"Dude, what the heck?"

"I wonder...Maybe if we shift into flying creatures we can just go above them."

"Sounds like a good idea."

"But then they might see us as even more of a threat. I don't know about you, but I'd rather not spend a lot of time fighting a horde of owls right now. Bigger fish and all. Yikes, excuse the mixed metaphors."

Without warning, the wall of owls parted and a strange beast approached, a sort of were-owl: a huge avian head atop a feathered, humanoid body, its legs bent like a bird's and ending in enormous talons, its arms vast wings that presently hung somewhat like a feathered cape. It jerked forward with a strange strutting step and regarded them, hostility and violence in its eyes.

"Ah, hell, no." Johnny took his own owl feather in his hand.

"Johnny, no, don't antagonize the..."

As usual, he didn't listen to her. Instead he shifted partially, imitating the being's form to a great degree.

"You're not the only one with a sharp beak, bro," he muttered gutturally.

"Foolish shifter," replied the were-owl with a hollow, reedy voice. "I have worn this form for longer than your weak race has walked the earth, ever since the Third Age, when rains of flame effaced the world. Do you actually expect I will be in the slightest intimidated by your mocking me?"

"Probably not, but just so you know, I'm not intimidated by how super old you are, dude. Who freaking cares if you've been eating bird seed for a million years? I'll still kick your feathered butt if you don't get out of the way."

"For what purpose do you approach *Chicunamictlan*?"

Johnny laughed. "*Chicano Mictlan? Qué onda, homie*...is this where *raza* go when they die?"

"Insolent gib, speak not with disrespect of *Chicunamictlan*, the mighty Halls of Death."

"So that's the name of the fortress?" Carol broke in, trying to diffuse the tension.

"Indeed. Within its dark, blood-tinged depths, souls find their final extinction. But you are living humans, and you cannot pass."

"Oh, yeah?" Johnny's voice was a snarl. "And who's going to stop us, huh?"

"I am Prince Muan, chief among the Tlatlacatecolo, Keeper of Mictlantecuhtli's Strigine Brigade."

"Huh? Chief among the *tacos locos*? Keeper of the grimy braids?" Johnny turned to Carol. "Can you translate?"

She sighed. "He takes care of the owls."

"Ah." He made a dismissive motion with one wing. "Man, you dudes need to tune into TV shows or surf the Internet or something. You talk like dead people. Oh, sorry, that's right."

Visibly controlling himself, Prince Muan spread his wings slightly. "You have yet to respond to my question. What brings you to this place?"

Carol didn't wait for Johnny to smart off again. "We're here for our mother. She's in there," she motioned with her head toward the fortress, "so that's where we're going. We've crossed all the required obstacles, Prince Muan, and I'm pretty sure that means we get an audience with Lord and Lady Death. So…if you'll just have your brigade get out of our way, we'll go talk to them."

"Impossible, wench. They are presently indisposed. Governing the Underworld is no child's game, understand. They have not the time to entertain the sniveling requests of every…"

"**Let them approach.**"

Two voices, in unison, uttered the words with enough volume that the parliament of owls actually shook, their feathers ruffled by the force of their rulers' command. The voices were spectral and monstrous, utterly inhuman and creaking with hoarse and eldritch harmonics that no twelve-year-old should ever have to hear. Carol's mind buckled at the mere thought of looking on the beings who had spoken.

Muan ducked his head in obeisance. "As you please, Great Ones. Jolom, Chabi…move aside. The two of you as well, Juraqan and Kaqix."

The screech owls that had blocked their way wheeled off to dusky recesses in the crystalline walls of Chicunamictlan. Prince Muan made a sweeping gesture with his right wing. "Proceed. If your offerings do not satisfy my sovereigns, we will have occasion to speak one final time before I feast on your eyes."

"Okay, that wasn't awkward." Johnny smirked as he returned to his human form. "Come, Carol. Let's leave this loser behind us."

They crossed the remaining distance between them and the entrance, around which scenes of death had been etched into the crystals. Bats flitted in and out of the darkness, twittering and diving at black beetles. Carol, having worn the form of a *kamasotzob*, felt no fear of them, but she took her brother's proffered hand all the same, and they stepped across the threshold.

Inky blackness surrounded her, so she shifted just her eyes and let her wolf vision pierce the dark. They were proceeding along a corridor whose shape and dimensions varied unpredictably: at times the ceiling loomed yards above them; at others, it was just centimeters away. The walls closed in at them and then receded.

"No human mind designed this crazy place," Johnny muttered, glancing at her with feline eyes.

"No, an ancient, sociopathic god did. And he's got our mom."

Johnny just grunted in reply, for the corridor had come to an end, emptying into a staggeringly cavernous hall lit by blue will-o'-the-wisps hanging suspended in the air. Ranged along the sides, standing at the ready between unevenly spaced stalagmites, were hundreds of skeletons, each clutching a spear, club or scythe. Their eyes glowed with the same blue fire that flickered above. Several turned their skulls to regard Carol, and the nape of her neck prickled with fear. But, the garrison of *calacas* only worried her for a moment. In the distance she could dimly see two figures.

"**Come closer,**" they urged in frightening voices. Snakes and scorpions skittered frantically across the floor at the sound.

Gripping Johnny's hand more tightly, Carol kept putting one foot in front of the other. She slipped her free fingers into her pocket and felt for the bag of jewels. *Oh, thank God. The sooner we get this over with, the better.*

Having faced the Ajalob, she thought she would be prepared for Lord and Lady Death. She was not. The closer she came to them, the more oppressed she became by thick, swirling *cehualli*, as if the sovereigns of Mictlan exuded that dark magic. Her stomach twisted into knots at the sickly sweet smell of blood and flowers.

The rulers of the Underworld struck real horror in her soul.

Seated on thrones molded from human bones, Lord and Leady Death loomed gigantic, nearly twice the height of a normal man and woman. He was gaunt and gray, his parchment skin pulled taut across wiry muscles and his abdomen so deeply sunken Carol could make out the outline of his spine. He wore a simple breechcloth, white with a single blue line at the fringed red edge, which was clearly dripping blood. His gnarled, thin legs were bare, but his splayed feet were fitted with black sandals. Draped across his shoulders was a *tilma* cape, bone white with the same turquoise stripe and fringe as his breechcloth. The cape was spattered with blood, which formed mind-twisting patterns as Carol stared. Around his neck was a yoke necklace of silver and turquoise from which small, gold-plated human skulls hung. Above this yoke, the skin of his lower jaw had been peeled away, exposing the bone. Though the rest of his face had flesh, it had worn thin and rotted in places, and his eyes were glowing red points in a circle of black. Atop his skull sat an extravagant headdress, formed of owl feathers and silver. From each side jutted a vicious-looking spike.

His companion was a more familiar sight to Carol, though not less frightening as a result. She wore a red *huipil* blouse and skirt, and around her neck was a chain from which dangled human hands and skulls, small enough that Carol suspected they belonged to children. Her face was a fleshless skull over which she had draped a black mantle that extended past her knees. It glittered with silver stars. In one bony hand she grasped a black orb; in the other, a sickle.

La Santísima Muerte, thought Carol. *Dressed like a twisted copy of the Virgin of Guadalupe, a mockery of Tonantzin.* She'd seen the image tattooed on arms and legs, displayed on t-shirts and truck windows. Not just an Aztec deity, Godmother Death was worshipped in the 21st century in the twins' own home town by people whose lives skirted the edge of normalcy, people for whom danger and death were occupational hazards.

I wonder if they'd be so eager to kneel to her if they were standing right here.

On the high backs of the thrones perched owls and bats. Before the Lord and Lady stood an obsidian basin. Between them, some ten yards away, a narrow archway led to the unknown bowels of the Underworld.

Johnny stood still holding on loosely to Carol's hand. Thankfully, it seemed he had no desire for sarcasm.

Raising long, thin fingers tipped with black claws, the Lord of Death pointed to the twins. "**Behold, breathing children. Having overcome every obstacle, you stand before us, we who** bear the titles Mictlantecuhtli and Mictecacihuatl, King and Queen of Mictlan. You seek admittance to the deepest heart of our realm."

Carol stammered. "Y-y-yes."

"These are not questions, living girl," Lady Death hissed. "Forbear speaking until you are commanded."

Mictlantecuhtli continued. "Your purpose here is known to us. We shall not interfere with your quest, as its object is also living and therefore anathema to Mictlan. The Dark One awaits you, and you will either win passage out of our realm or be destroyed utterly. First, you must satisfy *our* requirements. Have you gifts with which to pay our toll?"

Swallowing heavily, Carol drew the little leather bag from her pocket and, releasing her brother's hand, walked to the basin in front of Lord Death's towering throne of bone. Pulling loose the drawstring, she poured the contents into the stone receptacle; the rubies, diamonds, emeralds, sapphires and amethysts shined brightly and made a tinkling sound that felt distinctively out of place in that dark hall.

Stepping back, she stared expectantly up at that giant, horrible face, choking back bile at the rank smell of rot that Mictlantecuhtli exuded. The ruler of the Underworld nodded once, satisfied.

"You may pass, Carolina Garza."

"What...what about my brother?"

"He must pay his own price."

Johnny finally spoke. "But I lost my gems..."

Godmother Death snarled in disgust. "Then you must offer other tender, churlish knave. Tax not our patience."

Johnny grimaced and unslung his shield. "This belonged to Huitzilopochtli. It's got to be valuable. I'll hand it over to you."

"**Nothing stolen can you use, living boy.**" The black orb twisted like a living thing in her hand.

"Then what I am supposed to offer, huh? You want the cape? You want me to rescue my mom in my birthday suit, *cochina*?"

"**Imbecile. I care not for baubles or bits of rock. There is something precious to me, however, flowing through your very veins. If you would pass between these thrones, you must spill some of your blood.**"

Carol's stomach dropped. "No. No, Johnny, don't. There's got to be another way."

"Don't worry, sis. I'll be alright. It's just a little blood. I'll shift, heal, and be good as new." He got closer to the stone basin and looked up at the spectral queen of the dead. "So how does this work?"

In answer, she leapt from her throne and, suspended in the air above him, slashed at his left arm with her sickle, opening a long gash from wrist to elbow. Her orb floated free as she seized his hand with bony fingers and directed the flow of blood into the stone receptacle.

"Christ! That freaking hurt, you...you..." Johnny stared at the rising level of red. "That's enough, no? Let go of me already!"

Carol, without thinking, moved to intervene but Mictecacihuatl released her brother before she had a chance to confront the goddess. Johnny collapsed to the floor, his face white.

"Shift, Johnny, shift!"

His body jerked and twisted, and soon the jaguar lay before her, growling weakly. Struggling to all fours it bared its teeth at Lady Death.

"Save your crude insults for your own mother, knave. She deserves them more. Be that as it may, you have paid the toll. Begone with you."

Twitching his tail in anger, Johnny padded between the thrones and passed through the archway. Carol followed, eager to put the skeletal sovereigns behind her, desperate to see her mother again.

CHAPTER EIGHTEEN

ohnny slouched his way along the dark stones of the corridor the Black Road had become. He felt dizzy and weak, but he refused to let Carol see how drained he really was. *She needs me strong.* Mom *needs me strong.* When the time came, he figured he would be able to draw on the savage magic to sustain him. In the meanwhile, he would simply fake it.

Before long, the corridor ended at another chamber, a large cave-like structure with shallow pools of mineral water interspersed among stalagmites and other formations. At the center of the chamber lay a large obsidian mirror like the one the Little People had used to send the twins to Mictlan, but marred by a network of fine cracks that covered its surface like a snarled cobweb.

A way out?

Thoughts of escape, however, were interrupted by the sight of his mother, just a few yards from the mirror. His heart almost shattered as his animal eyes took in her brutalized form. She had a stone yoke around her neck, and a strange, glittering rope or cable ran like a lead from the yoke to a stalagmite. She was still dressed in the paint-speckled jeans and sleeveless blouse she'd been wearing on the day she disappeared. Her dark hair was tangled and matted, her face smeared with grime. Her eyes widened as she saw her daughter standing beside the jaguar.

"*Mamá!*" Carol shouted, and the two of them rushed to her side. Johnny shifted into human form and threw his arms around her. With shuddering sobs, she hugged them tightly.

"Oh, my beautiful children. How...how did you find me?"

"It was the Little People," Carol explained. "They used their *chay abah*, a mirror like that one, to send us through."

Johnny's mother reached up and laid a palm on each of his cheeks. "My sweet boy...You're a *nagual*, yes?"

"Yeah. So is Carol." He touched the stone yoke, anger flooding his heart. "And we've got the *xoxal*, Mom. So don't worry."

He stepped back out of her embrace and partially shifted into a crocodile. Then, his joy and rage mingling in the deepest regions of his soul, Johnny pulled up enough savage magic to close his jaws around the yoke and shatter it.

Verónica Quintero de Garza stood, staring at him dumbfounded. Johnny shifted back. He checked his mother's neck to make sure she wasn't too badly bruised or cut and Carol stroked her hair and brushed the dust from her clothes, trying to help her feel more herself.

"Children, I am so happy to see you again," their mother said once she had gotten over the shock of seeing her son become a were-croc, "but we need to leave this place before Tezcatlipoca returns. He orchestrated this, you understand. *Los quiere aquí,* wants both of you in this chamber with me. I don't know why, but let's not stay and find out."

Carol looked around. At the far end of the chamber was another opening, leading who-knew-where. "Well, we can't go back the way we came, so..."

"I was actually thinking we could use the mirror," Johnny said.

"But we don't know the chant," Carol pointed out.

"No, but we've got like savage magic and stuff, Carol. Let's try to focus on the obsidian, see if we can't make it start smoking and so on."

Their mother shook her head. "No, Juan Ángel. That's the passageway the Dark Lord uses. I'm pretty certain it doesn't lead back to our world. At least, not any good place in our world. *Olvídalo.*"

"*Pero, ma, si intentáramos…*"

"I said forget it, *m'ijo*. Seriously. It doesn't matter how powerful you think you've become, my love. You are *not* ready to face a powerful god. We need to go, now, before…"

The mirror trembled, and the three of them turned to stare at it. Smoke began curling from the cracks, as if a fire had been kindled beneath it. Strengthening this impression, strange glints of phosphorescence seemed to eddy in the mirror's depths. But then the surface of the mirror bulged, rippling upward as if something *within* it were pushing out. *Like Freddy in the old* Nightmare on Elm Street *films.* Then it was as if the surface of the mirror tore, and an impossibly enormous black-spotted paw thrust itself into the air, bending and stretching forward to sink vicious ebony talons into the rocky dirt.

"Run!" their mother screamed. Johnny grabbed her hand and dashed toward the passageway, but stalagmites burst upward from the ground behind them to create a wall. Another massive paw ripped through the mirror with an audible groan, as if the very fabric of the world had been rent apart by its grappling claws.

Carol pointed at the other side of the mirror, where fewer obstructions blocked the way. The three of them ran around the base of the *chay abah*. Johnny kept his eyes on the emerging forelegs of the dread beast, which tensed as if against some great weight. With an agonizing howl that thrummed through the mineral ceiling and sent a shower of red dust raining against Johnny's head and back, an indescribably huge jaguar erupted from the mirror, smoke curling from its rippling flesh as it snarled and shook itself. It slammed its paw down in their path, blocking their exit.

The ears of the jaguar, twitching this way and that, nearly scraped the chamber's high dome, and its tail slapped angrily against the farthest wall, knocking loose shiny mineral cascades. The rocky earth recoiled against the touch of three of its deadly paws, causing them to sink deep in the ground; the fourth still trapped within the mirror, which was now as glowing and smoky as an awakening fumarole.

Leaning its great head down to with arm's reach of Johnny, the jaguar opened unspeakable, slavering jaws to reveal teeth the length of a man's leg and a gullet that glistened darkly with ominous implications. A rumbling growl was born in the depths of this black mountain, building toward a crescendo.... But the growl, unexpectedly, became a voice: a voice like the fulminating roar, but speaking in words Johnny could understand. The jaguar was addressing them in Spanish, antiquated and replete with difficult words, but intelligible nonetheless.

"Have I your attention, humans?" It turned its fiery eyes on Johnny. **"Do you understand me, *boy*?"**

The voice was all around him, echoing in the air, trembling in the ground, whispering in the very depths of his soul. He had heard that voice many times before in his darkest dreams. There was no choice but to answer it.

"Uh, yes."

"Good. I have been awaiting you for some time. We have much to discuss. First, however, let me assume a less theatrical form."

The great jaguar began to shudder, its limbs twitching. Then, heaving and pulsing, its flesh began to shrink and run together, gradually taking on another form. Though still imposing, the beast was now a giant of a man, standing a half a meter above the tallest Johnny had ever seen. The skin of a jaguar was draped around him like a robe, its head hooding him and enfolding his handsome pale face in shadows. Behind his head, inexplicably floating in space, smoked a black mirror, made, as far as Johnny could tell, from obsidian. The young man was reminded for a moment of Catholic icons, saints with their circles of light. Except this was a circle of darkness, absolute and purest night. The man wore a gray tunic beneath the robe, decorated with black and gray feathers collected from, Johnny noted, crows and ravens and vultures. His right foot was shod in a sandal, but his left leg tapered to bare bone just above the ankle, and the skeletal left foot appeared to be caught within the slightly convex surface of the mirror that still smoldered on the cave floor.

"If you have not yet guessed, I am Tezcatlipoca, boy. Enslaver of Men. Master of Earth and Sky. Enemy of Both Sides. Omnipresent Darkness. I effect change, pull down the old ways in favor of stronger ones, destroy the weak. I existed before this world's beginning, and I shall be here at its end. An end, I

should add, that will come very soon, now that you two have begun to wield the savage magic."

Johnny's hands curled into fists. His heart beat wildly, almost painfully in his chest. "If you think," he panted, "that we're going to help you destroy the universe, then you must be out of your freaking mind. Or maybe you've been chewing on some funky cactus, huh?"

"Johnny," Carol breathed in a nervous warning. His mother gripped his hand tightly. He ignored them both.

"Yeah, no, you had our mom captive for six months. Our dad nearly lost it. Carol and I were pushed to our limits. You basically screwed our family, big time. So, you peg-legged freak, get the hell out of our way before you get a taste of the savage magic you're so excited about."

A grin spread across Tezcatlipoca's face, baring his feral teeth. "**You have summed up perfectly, if somewhat inelegantly, the very seed of your enslavement to me. That you are too young or stupid to understand only adds to my enjoyment of your predicament. In any event, *please*. Please make me get out of your way. I have been looking forward to this moment eagerly, boy.**"

Johnny could only focus on the word *enslavement*. A growl rose from deep within him, as if his *tonal* itself were responding to the dark god's taunts.

"Me too, you scabby old gib."

"Johnny, stop." His mother's voice was as firm and determined as ever. He couldn't help obeying her. "He's goading you. Don't fall into his trap."

"Your mother is very wise, boy. But very mortal. I think I will kill her now. Attempt to stop me, if you dare."

Verónica Quintero de Garza dropped to her knees, clutching at her throat and gasping. Pulling away from his mother and sister with a growl, Johnny shifted into the massive harpy eagle and launched himself at Tezcatlipoca, razor-sharp talons raking at the god's face. The dark lord leaned out of the way swiftly, reaching up a powerful hand to seize Johnny's legs and fling him toward the cavern floor. Beating mighty wings desperately, he barely managed to avoid slamming brutally against jagged rock.

"Ah, combat. It has been ages since anyone was stupid enough to attack me. Thank you, boy. It will be a genuine pleasure to grind your mortal flesh against the bare rock of Mictlan."

A gust of fire rushed at Tezcatlipoca then, and as the god turned to deflect it, Johnny rushed at him, sinking his talons into the god's shoulders. The dark lord grunted and reached back to grab at Johnny, but Carol, in fire serpent form, flung herself through the air, slamming into Tezcatlipoca and curling about him. Johnny began to pound his beak against the god's skull over and over as his sister started to squeeze.

"Impressive," Tezcatlipoca grunted. Then he simply wasn't there. Johnny and Carol dropped hard, hitting the mirror with a crunching thud. Above them, black smoke coalesced into the form of the god, smiling down at them. Then Tezcatlipoca took hold of both their heads and slammed them repeatedly against the ceiling before tossing them casually to either side of the cavern. Johnny, pain exploding within him, felt consciousness slipping, but he held on.

Too much blood loss, he thought weakly at his sister. *I can't react fast enough.*

Carol didn't respond. He could barely see her in the shadows of the rocks where she'd fallen. Her hair covered her face. *Probably unconscious, shifted back.*

Tezcatlipoca had turned his attention to their mother, who was attempting to run toward Carol.

"I promised you would be a witness and a tool in your children's destruction, did I not? Be still, then, and behold."

Verónica Quintero de Garza was jerked into the air by some invisible force and then violently hurled downward. Johnny gave a startled cry and dropped back into human form, frantically grabbing at his bracelet, searching for...*there.* A strand of Huitzilopochtli's hair. Gripping it between his thumb and index finger, Johnny shifted.

The transformation was dizzying. Power like he had never felt trembled along semi-divine limbs, and knowledge of how to use it rose almost instinctively within his mind. Reaching out a pale-blue hand, he called his shield to him, and it hurtled toward his outstretched arm like an obedient hunting hawk.

"Leave my mother alone, you bastard!" he shouted as he flung dark energy at Tezcatlipoca. The Lord of Chaos turned and smiled, spreading wide his arms at the attack. Johnny sent wave after wave of hate-driven, angry black magic pounding against him, but the god absorbed it all.

"Wonderful! You have delivered yourself to me so utterly that I can scarce believe your naïveté. I should have guessed you would ignore all sense, but for you to transform into my very protégé, the creature whose life was sustained by lore he

learned from me...the irony is simply delicious. Now, slave, feel my mastery of you and despair."

The cavern went dark and silent, as if filled with a spiritual sludge that even now tried to force its way into Johnny's mind and heart. Panicked, he began to push back with all the strength he possessed but it wasn't enough. Like grappling fingers, the *cehualli* poked through his defenses, found a hold and pried open a hole. A black quiet poured into him that was worse than any nightmare his sister had ever faced. Fleeing the *absence* that tried to consume him, Johnny retreated into himself.

"Yes, very astute. Cede control to me, boy. Sit back and watch as I wreak havoc with your own hands."

Johnny-as-Huitzilopochtli reached up with his free hand and snapped a stalactite off the ceiling. It was like being a marionette. His limbs moved against his volition. His demigod body took several steps toward his mother, arms cocking the stalactite back like a baseball bat. His eyes focused on the woman at his feet. He felt a sick smile spread across his corpse-blue face.

No!

"Oh, yes. She will die by your hand, boy."

Johnny gave a wordless howl of frustration. Clinging to his *tonal*, he reached deep, tapped the savage magic, channeled it against Tezcatlipoca's *cehualli* intrusion. The god redoubled, tripled the strength of his magical puppeteering. Desperate, Johnny dug in his soul, frantically sweeping away everything that impeded the flow of *xoxal*: memories, emotions, identity. He became an unthinking conduit through which the savage magic swept like a massive flood, ripping at the foundations of his very self.

Blue energy erupted like a geyser from his flesh, knocking

Tezcatlipoca down, ripping through the rock above their heads, tunneling upward through the roots of the World Tree to bore like a laser into the starry sky far above.

"YES!" Tezcatlipoca shouted, triumphant. **"Let it flow, Boy! Tear open a hole in heaven and let the end BEGIN!"**

The boy was a beacon. Power burned him clean of anything else but this. He saw the woman, twisted on the ground. He saw the girl, lifting herself up on her elbows, eyes full of tears. He saw the universe buckle. Soon it would crack. The boy saw no reason for it not to. Let it crack. Let it burn. Let darkness fall forever.

Then a small voice whispered. The boy ignored it, but it was insistent. Over and over it whispered a phrase. He listened, hoping that his attention would silence it.

At the end, remember who you are.

The boy thought for a moment. He could not remember who he was. He was the beacon, the conduit, the tool. That was all.

The most important gift. It already lies within you.

But what was the gift? The boy had no idea. He did not know who he was. He had been burned clean of any gifts.

The universe groaned, ready to split asunder.

And then came a song. A beautiful, beautiful song, sung in bereft but loving tones by a familiar voice.

> *¡Oh madre querida!*
> *¡Oh madre adorada!*
> *Que Dios te bendiga,*
> *aquí en tu morada.*
>
> *Que Dios te conserve,*
> *mil años de vida,*

feliz y dichosa,
¡oh madre querida!

Sí estás dormidita,
escucha este canto,
que todos tus hijos,
convierten en llanto.

Tú que por tu hijos,
vives implorando,
en ti madrecita,
vivimos pensando.

Recibe el cariño,
de todos tus hijos,
que nunca en la vida,
podrán olvidarte.

Sí estás escuchando,
podrás alegrarte,
que todos tus hijos,
vienen a cantarte.

Tú nombre es María,
y no hallan que darte,
se sienten dichosos,
al felicitarte.

And with a shuddering rush, the boy recognized his mother, the woman who had loved him more than anyone for as long as he had lived. She had given him his name, and she would whisper it to him every night, thinking him asleep. *Te quiero, Juan Ángel. Tu madre te quiere mucho.*

"I remember who I am," he muttered wonderingly, looking at Tezcatlipoca, whose smile began to fade. "I'm Juan Ángel Garza. Son of Verónica and Oscar. Brother of Carolina. And the gift I already have...it's their love. Their *love*. And...the love I feel for them. You can't touch that, can you?"

Tezcatlipoca stood but said nothing. Taking the love Carol's singing had awakened, Johnny shut off the savage magic. Dropping the stalactite, he shifted back into human form and tossed the shield aside.

"Kill us if you want," he said quietly. "But I'm not going to help you destroy the universe. You lose, freak. Game over."

Tezcatlipoca stared at him wordlessly for a moment. Then he drew his hands out from beneath the jaguar robe. In his right he gripped a long, curved obsidian knife. Johnny looked down at his mother, knelt beside her. She was still breathing. Carol, pulling her t-shirt back on, crouched beside him and smiled sadly.

"Thanks," he told her, reaching for her hand.

She nodded. Looking over his shoulder at Tezcatlipoca, she addressed the dark god. "We're ready. Get it over with."

His laugh was not unexpected. Johnny ignored it, stroking his mother's tangled hair. *Soon we'll find out what our path to Beyond is, Mom. The three of us, together.*

Moments stretched into minutes. Unexpectedly, the thrumming of the mirror began, and Johnny turned to see Tezcatlipoca activating his portal.

"I see by the look in your eyes that you are utterly bewildered. Good. My faith in your stupidity is not unfounded, I see. You believe that I have lost, that this 'game' has concluded. Eventually you will comprehend that everything that

has occurred has been according to my plan. I have orchestrated your every step."

Johnny quailed inwardly, but scoffed and spat. "Whatever. You almost brought about the star demon apocalypse or whatever. We shut you down. Period."

"Foolish boy. Do you not understand that you would have been destroyed by so much *xoxal* long before you could have broken open the Tzitzimime's prison? You are not strong enough to fulfill the destiny I have prepared for you. But you are much closer than you were scant days ago. With time I will shape you, boy, into precisely the tool I require. And when you are ready, I plan to wield you effortlessly. In fact, I suspect you will beg me to use you to bring about the end of this world that my brother so stupidly strives to preserve. You will turn your back on him, on your sister, on your parents, and willingly aid me."

Johnny stood, his eyes stinging. "It'll...it'll be a cold day in hell..." he began.

"Indeed it will." Tezcatlipoca pulled his jaguar cape tight about him and stepped into the smoking mirror, disappearing in a black swirl.

In the silence that followed, Johnny turned to Carol, tears streaming down his face.

"Never. You hear me? *Never*. I'll kill myself first. And if I can't, you're going to have to, Carol."

CHAPTER NINETEEN

Carol balked at her brother's request. *I couldn't ever kill him. Not even if he were about to destroy the planet.* When she'd seen him standing there, that column of blue light bursting from his transformed body, the shape of Huitzilopochtli that he had so stupidly assumed, she had felt only fear for him. She loved him too much to do anything but try to bring him back with her *cuicuani* singing magic. The thought of using her abilities to end his life...it was impossible.

"No one," their mother breathed, "is going to kill anyone. Not even themselves."

She shifted briefly into her jaguar form to heal her wounds, and then she became human again. Her hair hung straight and long, and her skin glowed beautifully. Sitting up, she brushed dust from her blouse.

"That monster kept me from shifting for months. I feel much better now. Still could use a hot shower, *pero ni modo.*"

They helped her to her feet. Johnny ducked his head in shame.

"Mom, I'm sorry. *Perdóname.*"

"Shh. *Ya.* We're all fine now."

"But you heard what he said," Johnny whispered. "He planned all of it. And he's going to do more. He's going to make me..."

She put two fingers against his lips, silencing him. "He can't make you do anything you don't want to, Juan Ángel. And when it comes time to face him again, you won't be alone. There are many people that fight his schemes. You are in good company, I promise you."

Carol felt weirdly jealous. *Why didn't Tezcatlipoca attack me with cehualli? Why was he so totally focused on Johnny? Is it...because I'm a girl? That's really stupid.*

Johnny seemed to sense her jumbled-up emotional state. "Carol, I think he knew he could make me snap faster, you know? That's why he focused all his attention on me. And he knew you are my balance, so he tried knocking you out. Doesn't know how stubborn you can be, though. Thanks." His eyes went serious but soft. "I would've burned myself out from the inside. I had no control. But you sang for me, Sis. You made me focus on Mom and stuff. You saved me."

Without warning, he threw his arms around her and squeezed. "Thanks," he muttered thickly into her hair. Carol hugged him back.

"Okay," she said, looking at her mother. "What's next?"

"Well, we need to get out of here."

"Like Carol said, we can't go back," Johnny warned.

"I know. So..." Their mother gestured at the opening in the far wall. A dark path made its way to the threshold and beyond. "Let's see what's at the very center, kids."

The passageway they entered was brief. It opened onto an even vaster chamber ceilinged in living wood. *The World Tree,* Carol realized. *We're right beneath it.*

There were three other passageways that debouched into the

cavern, and from each a different path emerged: red, green, white. All the paths, including the black one they had been following, converged at the center of the chamber, which was dominated by an enormous stone-lipped well that coruscated with light from deep within and illuminated the entire space with a dappled glow. As Carol watched, dozens of brilliant, sparkling masses came streaming along each path and poured themselves into the roiling luminosity at the very heart of Mictlan.

"They're souls, no?" Johnny muttered. "Passing Beyond. Everything Tezcatlipoca made people fear is a lie. They aren't destroyed. He can't snuff them."

Carol heard something then. Tilting her head, she tried to listen more closely.

"¿Qué pasa, amor?" her mother asked. "Are you okay?"

"Don't you hear that? It's...music."

The portals of her soul opened, and the song rolled in on majestic swells of sweet bliss. There were no words. It was a hymn of completion, of satisfaction, of long-needed rest. *Hope, she felt. And love. Eternal epiphany. Unity. Peace.*

Dropping to her knees, she stared at the well, overcome.

"What?" Johnny asked, crouching beside her, worry on his face. "What's wrong?"

She looked at him and smiled. "Nothing, Johnny. Nothing's wrong. Everything's going to be fine. No matter what comes. We'll all be okay."

Her mother tousled her hair lovingly and looked around. "I'm not sure what road we should take, kids. Any suggestions?"

"I'd opt for the Green Road, were I you."

Carol lifted her eyes. Walking through the entrance along the green path was Xolotl in his human form. His blue eyes twinkled in the shimmering light. Souls streamed past him on either side.

"Nice of you to join us," Johnny said with a smirk. "I mean, I guess I understand. Mrs. Four-in-One told us you couldn't make it through Xibalba. But, man, we sure could've used some help."

"Johnny," muttered Carol. "That's not fair. We had lots of help."

"And the rest you handled splendidly." Xolotl gestured for them to approach him. Carol stood and the three walked in a semicircle around the Well of Souls. "You were incredible. Despite all that assailed you, you held fast to your own identities and to the love that makes your family strong. You are truly heroes, my children, and we are proud of your steadfastness."

"Yeah, uh, we also kicked some major butt," Johnny added with a half-smile as they reached Xolotl's side.

"That you did, Juan Ángel. That you did."

Their mother was staring at the man with eyes wide. Carol noticed with surprise that her bottom lip was actually trembling.

"Are you...*Him*?"

Xolotl eyes grew soft, and he reached out to touch her head in a fatherly gesture. "No, Verónica. Or, rather, just a small part of him. But he sees you dear. And so does his mother. They're ever watchful."

Carol wasn't sure what the two of them meant, but there was little time for deciphering. Xolotl nodded firmly and turned away.

"We've a need for speed, so you'll have to cling tightly. Riding the Green can be...treacherous."

He shifted into his giant hound form, and Carol soon found herself boosted into place upon his broad back, her mother and brother behind her.

"Say goodbye to Mictlan, children. I suspect you'll never tread this realm again."

Scoffing, Johnny said, "Good riddance."

Their mother whispered something unintelligible.

Carol was silent, but as the massive dog began to run along the green path, through the strange caverns of Chicunamictlan, she thought she might not mind taking this road Beyond. At the very least, she hoped that Tezcatlipoca's hold on the place would loosen now so that its ancient function—preparing souls for the next stage—could continue in peace.

Then they were at the circular lake, and the water surged green and pure from the inky depths, lifting Xolotl high and bearing them at impossible speeds back along the Nine Deserts. Each of those levels of Mictlan became a blur beneath them, muted by speed and the foaming liquid. Carol clung tightly to Xolotl, burying her face in his short, red hair. Her mother's arms were about her. The wind whistled by loudly. It was impossible to hear anything, except the echoes of that haunting song that had risen from the Well of Souls.

Finally, the wave slowed and dipped, splashing broadly into the waters of Chignahuapan. Xolotl paddled the rest of the way to shore, where the Green Road terminated in the strange, roiling curtain that divided this dimension from theirs.

"I wish this could be the end of it for them," their mother said, somewhere between stern and hopeful. "Johnny is very worried about the lies Tezcatlipoca told him."

Xolotl nodded his shaggy head. "I understand. But they are

special. You knew it when they were born. We will work to protect them, to keep the struggle far away. But the Lord of Chaos has designs for them, and they must be prepared."

"I can prepare them," their mother said, nodding to herself. "I'll teach them everything my mother and the *tzapame* showed me."

"I had assumed nothing less. But, Verónica, you know nothing of the savage magic they can wield. No one does. Not I, not Tezcatlipoca, not Quetzalcoatl or the Blessed Mother. We have inklings of how it might be triggered, we understand its implications for this world, but we cannot use it directly. Even if were permitted to us, we do not have the lore required."

Carol could sense the frustration in her mother. The woman shook her head in disbelief. "Well, who does?"

Xolotl glanced upward. "You would have to ascend to uppermost branches of the World Tree, to Omeyocan itself, to find an answer to that question."

Johnny made a dismissive sound and smirk. "In other words, we're on our own."

"In terms of learning to wield *xoxal*, yes."

Carol felt impatience rising in her. She touched her mother's arm. "We'll figure it out together. But there'll be time for that. Can we please just go home? Dad's probably freaking out. *Tía* Andrea, too."

Verónica nodded. "So what do we do?"

Xolotl nudged the gray curtain with his muzzle. "Push through at this point. You'll emerge in the mountains again, close to Monterrey."

Carol reached out and touched the hound's short, red fur.

"Thank you, Xolotl. We owe you."

Their guide grinned. "Oh, the debt is mine, child. Ours. You have risen to the challenges and foiled the dark plans of chaos for a time. Now, go. Enjoy your lives. Love one another. Rejoice in the beauty of the world you've protected."

Johnny stepped toward the curtain, reaching back for his mother's hand. She grabbed a hold of him and clasped Carol's hand as well.

"Goodbye, Mictlan," Carol muttered. She felt the slightest inexplicable twinge of regret.

Then Johnny pushed through the gray, pulling them after him.

CHAPTER TWENTY

The world was assembling itself around them, but at the periphery of the gray, Johnny could sense a vast darkness in which enormous monsters seemed to writhe in a mass of serpentine coils, leathery wings, and endless hunger for destruction. Their attention coalesced momentarily, focusing on his awareness of them, but then he dropped into this world, stumbling across rocks on the sandy floor of a cave. His mother and sister emerged from the space between dimensions a split second later.

After the initial disorientation, Johnny became aware of a deafening roar that filled the small space, not so much a cave as an alcove. Water was rushing in torrents across the entrance to the small space.

"¿Qué fregados?" he exclaimed.

"I think we're at the Cola de Caballo," his mother shouted above the sound of the cascade. "Horsetail Falls. In Cumbres National Park."

She hugged them both excitedly and led them carefully through the rushing curtain of water. Down a rugged slope dotted with trees, the three of them made their way to the crowds of tourists visiting the famous waterfall. From there it was relatively easy to grab a taxi and let the warm air dry them as the driver wove his expert way through traffic to Colonia Tecno-lógico.

More difficult, however, was explaining to the police officers assigned to their missing persons case what had happened. Johnny was perversely proud of the lie his mother spun: she'd been kidnapped by *zetas* in Donna and taken across the border. The band's leader had gone missing, however, so the criminals had been awaiting further instructions for months. When they had finally sent their demands to her sister's apartment, the twins had intercepted the message and had foolishly gone off to rescue her, taking 50,000 of their aunt's pesos. The criminals had accepted the money and let them go.

The police didn't exactly buy this story, but they had little choice other than to accept it. Andrea confirmed the missing money and the twins corroborated every detail. Reporters swarmed the area, and Johnny almost broke down crying when he saw his mother quickly slap on make-up to be interviewed for the local news. It was such an ordinary ritual, but one he had missed more than he had imagined. *She's something else, isn't she?*

In the midst of all the chaos, the phone rang. Everyone was busy, so Johnny answered the old-fashioned landline.

"*¿Bueno?*"

"Johnny?" It was his father, his voice trembling excitedly.

"Dad?"

"Yes, son, it's me. Oh, God, I'm so glad you're okay. You scared the crap out of me, kid."

"I know, I know. But we got Mom back, Dad. She's here, right now, safe and sound. Andrea said she called and left a message for you."

There was a pause. His father's breath came in ragged

snatches. "Yeah, I heard it. Can I talk to her? To your mother?"

"Hang on…She's outside with a reporter. Let me go get her."

Johnny's mother rushed inside when he told her who was on the phone. After about five minutes, she hung up.

"He's on his way," his mother explained with a nervous smile. "He had been getting an import sticker for his car to drive down; that's why he didn't answer at first."

She was crying a little, and Johnny hugged her tightly. "We're going to be together again, Mom. All of us. Don't cry."

"But that's why I'm crying, *m'ijo*. I'd almost lost hope that I'd see any of you again. It's a miracle, and these are tears of gratitude to the Virgin. Now, go on, get cleaned up. Your father will be here in three hours or so. He's going to take us to visit your grandmother's grave, and then we'll head home."

Oscar Garza nearly swept his wife off her feet in the driveway when he arrived, dashing from the car and embracing her tightly. Johnny turned away as they kissed, more out of embarrassment than a desire to give them privacy, and then he and Carol hugged both of their parents. A few straggling photographers snapped away at their cameras, and the image of the reunited family would appear the following day on the front page of *El norte*.

Retelling the cover story on the drive to Saltillo made Johnny feel horribly guilty. *This is Dad*, he thought to Carol. *He's got a right to know the truth.*

Yeah, well, that's Mom's decision, Johnny. She'll tell him when the moment's right, I guess.

He didn't argue with her, but his father's pointed questions made it obvious the man knew something wasn't quite right. Oscar Garza didn't push too hard, though. Johnny figured he was just too relieved to have his family back together to pursue his suspicions.

Soon they were all four of them gathered around the gravestone of Helga Barrón de Quintero, which stood right beside that of her husband Ramón. Johnny's mother laid a wreath of marigolds upon the freshly turned earth and ran her fingers gently across the inscription carved into the granite cross: *Se alza como una leona.*

She rises like a lioness.

Johnny couldn't take it anymore. *Too many secrets. Lies. That's Tezcatlipoca's way. Not mine.*

He looked around carefully. The cemetery was empty of people.

"Dad, there's something important you need to know."

What are you doing, Johnny? Carol's thoughts were stern, tinged with panic.

He ignored her, stepped back from the grave, and shifted.

Come on, Carol, you too. Now.

She sighed and dropped into her wolf form. Their father stumbled backward, bumping into his father-in-law's tombstone.

"*Ah, cómo serán de tercos los dos,*" their mother muttered in irritation. Then she, too, morphed into a jaguar. The three *naguales* stood shoulder to shoulder, looking up at Oscar Garza.

Unexpectedly, he smiled and gave a nervous laugh.

"Well, that explains a lot," he said, reaching out to rub his shaking hand against the fur of each of them in turn. "And it means I'm not crazy after all. Wow. Garza family, we've got some important things to talk about."

The adventures of Johnny and Carol will continue in
A KINGDOM BENEATH THE WAVES,
GARZA TWINS: BOOK TWO,
coming in 2016

GUIDE TO PRONUNCIATION

Words in Spanish and Nahuatl (the human language that the Little People and inhabitants of Mictlan also speak) have similar pronunciation rules, so they are combined below..

Vowels

a—as in "father".

e—as in "bet".

i—as in "police".

o—as in "no".

u—as in "flute" (Spanish only).

Diphthongs (vowel combinations)

ai—like the "y" in "my".

au—like "ow" in "cow".

ei—like the "ay" in "hay" (Spanish only).

eu—a blend of "e" of "bet" and "u" of flute (Spanish only).

ia—like the "ya" of "yard" (Spanish only).

ie—like the "ye" of "yellow" (Spanish only).

io—like the "yo" of "yodel" (Spanish only).

iu—like "you" (Spanish only).

ua—like the "wa" in "want".

ue—like the "whe" in "where".

ui—like "we".

Consonants

b—as in "baby" (Spanish only).

c—like "k" before "a," "o" and "u"; like "s" before "e" and "i".

d—as in "dog" at the beginning of a word; like the "th" in "that" elsewhere (Spanish).

f—as in "four" (Spanish only).

g—like the "g" in "go" before "a," "o" and "u"; like "h" before "e" and "i" (Spanish).

h—silent before vowels; a glottal stop like the middle sound of "kitten" after vowels.

j—like "h," but harsher (Spanish only).

l—as in "like".

m—as in "moon".

n—as in "no".

ñ—roughly like the "ni" in "onion".

p—as in "pet".

r—like the "dd" in the American pronunciation of "ladder" (Spanish only).

s—as in "see" (Spanish only).

t—as in "ten".

v—like "b" in "baby" (Spanish only).

x—like "sh" in "she" (Nahuatl) or like "h" (Spanish only).

y—as in "yes".

z—like "s" in "see".

Digraphs (two letters always written together)

ch—as in "check".

cu/uc—"kw" as in "queen".

hu/uh—like "w" in "we".

ll—like "y" in "yes" (Spanish only).

qu—like "k" in "key".

rr—a "rolled r" (Spanish only).

tl—roughly like the "ttle" in "bottle".

tz—like the "ts" in "cats".

Note also that all Nahuatl (and most Spanish) words are stressed on the next-to-the-last syllable:

Mictecacíhuatl—mic/te/ca/CI/huatl.

Tezcatlipoca—tez/ca/tli/PO/ca.

Tonantzin—to/NAN/tzin.

Quetzalcoatl—que/tzal/CO/atl.

GLOSSARY

Acolmiztli—A black puma who leads the *Balamija* in the second level of Mictlan

Ahuiateteo—Gods of vice and excess.

ahuitzotl—(pl. ahuitzomeh) "Water dog," a sort of magical aquatic creature with a hand at the end of its tail.

Ajalob—The Lords of Xibalba.

Apanhuiayo—A putrid lake near the center of Mictlan in the ninth level.

Balamija—"Jaguar House," the tribe of jaguars and pumas that inhabit the second level of Mictlan. Also spelled Balamiha.

Black Road, the—One of four paths into the Underworld, the only one that living humans can use.

cehualli—See 'shadow magic"

Chalmecatl—A massive serpent guarding the entrance to the Underworld. Brother of Xochitonal. Also the name of one of the three Lords of the Green Quarter of Xibalba.

chay abah—A large obsidian mirror used to travel between realms.

Chicunamictlan—"The Halls of Death," the fortress at the center of Mictlan.

Chignahuapan—A vast and dangerous river that rings the Underworld (more properly "Chiucnahuapan" in Nahuatl)

Chipohyoh—Name given to Johnny Garza by the Balamija.

cuauhcualli—A sort of stone dungeon beneath the *Mitnal*.

Dark Lord, the—See "Tezcatlipoca".

Feathered One, the—See "Quetzalcoatl".

First Age, the—The era from the creation of the earth to its first destruction by Tezcatlipoca.

Fifth Age, the—The present era of history.

García Caves—A complex of caverns in the mountains of northern Mexico that leads to the realm of the Tzapame.

Huitzilopochtli—The god of war.

Itzeecayan—"Land of the Cold Razor Winds," the eighth level of the Underworld.

Itzocelotl—A black jaguar of the Balamija.

Ixcuinan—The Paradox, goddess of sin and forgiveness. Also known as Tlazolteotl.

Ixpuztec—A pterodactyl-like monster with the backward-bent legs of a rooster and a shattered, scarred, human-like face. Able to assume multiple forms to drive people to despair.

kamasotz—"Snatch-bat," a creature from the bowels of Mictlan.

Kisin—Speaker of the Ajalob and High Lord of Xibalba, capital city of Mictlan.

Kotzabalam—A were-jaguar from the second level of Mictlan, part of the Balamija.

Little People, the—Tzapame, a race of elf-like beings.

Lechuza—Large screech owl, often a nagual in owl form.

Lord of Chaos, the—See "Tezcatlipoca".

Lords of the Black Quarter—Three members of the Ajalob who govern a fourth of Xibalba: Ah Pukuh, Hunhau and Akan.

Lords of the Green Quarter—Three members of the Ajalob who govern a fourth of Xibalba: Chalmecatl, Chalmecacíhuatl, and Nexoxocho.

Lords of the Red Quarter—Three members of the Ajalob who govern a fourth of Xibalba: Yoaltecuhtli, Yoalcíhuatl and Tzontémoc.

Lords of the White Quarter—Three members of the Ajalob who govern a fourth of Xibalba: Techlotl, Cuezalli, and Itzcoliuhqui.

Malinalli Tenepal—Also Malintzin or Malinche, the indigenous princess whose knowledge had helped Hernán Cortes defeat the Aztecs.

Mictlan—See "Underworld, the."

Mictlantecuhtli—Lord of the Dead, ruler of the Underworld.

Mictecacíhuatl—Lady of the Dead, ruler of the Underworld.

Mitnal—the Council Chamber of the Ajalob.

Muan—A prince of the Underworld, chief among the Tlatlacatecolo, Keeper of Mictlantecuhtli's Strigine Brigade.

nagual(es)—Shapeshifter(s); also nahualli.

Nahualocelomeh—(s. nahualocelotl) "Were-jaguars," giants given shapeshifting ability by Tezcatlipoca.

nahualli—(pl. nahualtin) See "nagual".

Nextepehua—Prince of Ashes, a demon of the Underworld.

Nine Deadly Deserts, the—Different stages or levels of the Underworld (blackness, bats and jaguars, cold, haunted ruins, lava plains, ashes, heart-eating demons, obsidian winds and a putrid lake).

Pingo—One of the Little People; liaison with the Garza twins.

Quetzalcoatl—Lord of Creation and Order; brother of Tezcatlipoca.

sacred singer—Someone able to wield sacred song magic.

sacred song magic—Sorcery that uses singing to work spells.

shadow magic—The dark power of chaos wielded by Tezcatlipoca and his minions.

teocuicani—See "sacred singer".

teocuicayotl—See "sacred song magic".

teotl—Divine energy found in all living things.

Tepeme Monamictia—the "Crashing Mountains," a sort of perilous gateway into the Underworld (also *tepetl imonamiquiyan* or "place where the mountains crash").

Tepeyollotl—"Mountain Heart," the nahualli of Tezcatlipoca; a massive jaguar.

Tezcatlipoca—Lord of destruction and chaos; brother of Quetzalcoatl.

Tlatlacatecolo—"Man-owls," humanoid owls from the Underworld's lowest levels.

Tlecoatl—A wyrm under Huitzilopochtli's command.

tonalli—A secondary spirit formed from teotl; the animal soul of a nagual.

tonal—A nagual's animal soul.

Tonantzin—"Our Beloved Mother," the supreme goddess.

Tukumbalam—A giant shapeshifter from the second level of Mictlan who assumes jaguar shape as part of the Balamija.

tzapame—See "Little People, the".

tzapatzin—Singular form of tzapame.

tzitzimitl—(pl. tzitzimimeh) Star demon, a sort of destructive goddess capable of triggering an apocalypse.

Underworld, the—Mictlan, a nine-layered afterlife nestled among the roots of the World Tree presently controlled by Tezcatlipoca, though overseen by Lord and Lady Death.

Well of Souls, the—The place at the very heart of the Underworld where purified souls pass Beyond.

World Tree, the—The axis of the universe, joining Mictlan, the earth and the thirteen heavens.

wyrm—A dragon-like winged serpent.

Xibalba—The capital city of Mictlan.

Xiuhcoatl—The personal wyrm of Huitzilopochtli.

Xochitonal—A giant green lizard that guards the entrance to the Underworld. Brother of Chalmecatl.

Xolotl—The nahualli of Quetzalcoatl; exists separately from the god now, mostly in the form of a large dog, in Mictlan.

xoxal—Savage magic, a little-understood force possessed by twin shapeshifters.

GUIDE TO SPANISH WORDS, PHRASES AND SONGS

Chapter 1

m'ija—sweetie (literally "my daughter")

tía—aunt

Chapter 2

ven, m'ijo; ven acá—come, son; come here.

güey—dude

¿Qué te crees?—What do you think you are?

No me creo nada—I don't think I'm anything.

Conque hablas español, bolillo—So you speak Spanish, white dude.

Güero, sí—Light-skinned, sure.

ese—guy

vato—dude

sancho—lover, boyfriend (of a woman who is already married or spoken for)

se está volviendo loco—he's going crazy

imbécil—imbecile, idiot

Chapter 3

Ya veo—I see.

gringolizados—Americanized

café con leche—coffee made with milk

abuela—grandmother

tía—aunt

solterona—spinster, unmarried woman

puestos—vendor stands

cajón—drawer

Chapter 4

nagual—shapeshifter

tonal—shadow soul or animal soul

vayan—go (plural)

abue—grandma

mensa—dummy

depósito—small corner store

Gansitos—sort of chocolate snack cake

Chapter 5

norteño—genre of music with accordion

Nahuatl—the language spoken by the Aztecs

Chapter 6

que me abraces ya—put your arms around me now

Chapter 7

¿Qué?—What?

¡Hijo de su Pink Floyd!—nonsense saying along the lines of "son of a biscuit eater"

Chapter 8

fresa—prep; rich, stuck-up kid

Guácala—gross!

O sea, qué asco, en serio—I mean, how nasty, for real!

Chapter 9

Ah, que la...—incomplete interjection along the lines of "son of a..."

papi—daddy

Chapter 10

lechuza— screech owl

Chapter 11

Ya cállate, méndigo mapache—shut up already, you freaking raccoon

Chapter 12

esponjada—unduly upset (equivalent to "with your panties/undies in a bunch")

abuelita—granny

mis amores—my darlings

Han sido muy valientes, los dos—You have been very brave, both of you.

A la ru ru niño Off to sleep, my baby
A la ru ru ya. Off to sleep you go.
Tus sueños te protegen Your dreams will now protect you
De la oscuridad. From the dark unknown.

A la ru ru niño Off to sleep, my baby
A la ru ru ya, Off to sleep at once.
Porque viene el coco The boogeyman is coming
Y te comerá. And he'll eat you up.

Y si no te come, And if he doesn't eat you,

Él te llevará; He'll take you to his lair;

Y si no te lleva, And if he doesn't take you,

Quién sabe qué hará. Who knows what he will do.

Este lindo niño This sweet little baby

Ya se va a dormir Is ready now for bed.

Háganle la cuna Make a cradle for him

De rosa y jazmín. Of jasmine and of rose.

Toronjil de plata, Silvery lemon balm,

Torre de marfil, That drifts from ivory towers,

Arrullen al niño Lull my baby gently now,

Que ya quiere dormir. He's ready now for bed.

ven acá, amor — come here, love

Chapter 13

lucha libre — wrestling

Chapter 14

Allá en la fuente There in the fountain

había un chorrito, There was a geyser

se hacía grandote Big like a mountain

se hacía chiquito. Or small like a miser.

Estaba de mal humor — And, oh! it could be such a snot

pobre chorrito tenía calor. When that little geyser felt it was hot.

Chapter 15

chapopote — tar

Chapter 16

Órale—you betcha

Catrina—name of Godmother Death in Mexico

Chapter 17

lechuzas—screech owls

tecolotes—small owls

qué onda—what's up

raza—Mexican-American people

tacos locos—crazy tacos

calacas—skeletons

La Santísima Muerte—Godmother Death

cochina—dirty-minded woman

Chapter 18

Mamá—Mom

Los quiere aquí—He wants you here

Olvídalo—Forget it.

Pero, ma, si intentáramos…—But, Mom, if we tried…

¡Oh madre querida! Oh, beloved Mother!

¡Oh madre adorada! Oh, adorable Mother!

Que Dios te bendíga, May God bless you

aquí en tu morada. Here in your home.

Que Dios te conserve, May God keep you,

mil años de vida, Through a thousand years of life,

feliz y dichosa, Happy and lucky,

¡oh madre querida! Oh, beloved Mother!

Sí estás dormidita, If you're fast asleep,

escucha este canto, Listen to this song,
que todos tus hijos, The one your children
convierten en llanto. Transform into weeping.

Tú que por tu hijos, You who live praying
vives implorando, On your children's behalf,
en ti madrecita, It's you, dearest Mother,
vivimos pensando. That we live thinking of.

Recibe el cariño, Accept the affection
de todos tus hijos, Of all of your children
que nunca en la vida, Who could never, ever,
podrán olvidarte. Forget about you.

Sí estás escuchando, If you're listening,
podrás alegrarte, You can feel joy,
que todos tus hijos, Because all of your children
vienen a cantarte. Have come here to sing.

Tú nombre es María, Your name is Maria,
y no hallan que darte, And no gift is enough,
se sienten dichosos, We feel fortunate simply
al felicitarte. To congratúlate and praise you.

Te quiero, Juan Ángel. Tu madre te quiere mucho—I love you, Juan Ángel. Your mother loves you very much.

Chapter 19
pero ni modo—but, oh, well!
Perdóname—Forgive me
Ya—enough already
¿Qué pasa, amor?—What's the matter, dear?

Chapter 20

¿Qué fregados?—What the heck?

¿Bueno?—Hello?

Se alza como una leona—She rises like a lioness.

Ah, cómo serán de tercos los dos—Ah, you two just have to be stubborn.

A product of an ethnically diverse family with Latino roots, David Bowles has spent most of his life in the Río Grande Valley, where he presently lives and works. Recipient of awards from the American Library Association, the Texas Institute of Letters and the Texas Associated Press, he has written several books, among them *Border Lore* and the Pura Belpré Honor Book *The Smoking Mirror*.